That Day the
Rabbi Left Town

That Day the Rabbi Left Town

BY

HARRY KEMELMAN

FAWCETT COLUMBINE
NEW YORK

A Fawcett Columbine Book
Published by Ballantine Books
Copyright © 1996 by Harry Kemelman

All rights reserved under International
and Pan-American Copyright Conventions. Published in the
United States by Ballantine Books, a division of Random House, Inc., New York,
and simultaneously in Canada by Random House
of Canada Limited, Toronto.

Library of Congress Cataloging-in-Publication Data
Kemelman, Harry.
That day the Rabbi left town / by Harry Kemelman.—1st ed.
p.   cm.
ISBN 0-449-91002-4
1. Small, David (Fictitious character)—Fiction. 2. Rabbis—Massachusetts—Fiction.
I. Title.
PS3561.E398T48   1996

813'.54—dc20   95-36074
                                                                      CIP

Manufactured in the United States of America
First Edition: February 1996
10 9 8 7 6 5 4 3 2 1

That Day the
Rabbi Left Town

Chapter 1

I⊤ was the middle of May and unusually hot for the season as Rabbi David Small of the Barnard's Crossing Temple made ready for his appointment with President Macomber of Windermere College in Boston's Back Bay. He presented himself to his wife, Miriam, for inspection.

"You're going like that? Without a tie?"

"It's a hot day."

"But you're going to be interviewed for a job," she protested.

"So what? These days professors lecture in their shirtsleeves and blue jeans."

"But you're not going to lecture. You're going to see the president for a job."

"All right, so I'll put on a tie." He went up the stairs to the bedroom closet.

But she accompanied him to the bedroom to pass on his selection. Although she was fifty years old, Miriam looked like a schoolgirl. Her blond hair, occasionally "touched up" by the hairdresser, was piled up on top of her head as if to get it out of the way. Only the determined set of her chin in her heart-shaped face, and the fine lines at the corners of her eyes, showed her age. Her husband, the rabbi, at fifty-three, did show his age. His dark hair was streaked with gray. He wore thick-lensed glasses that he would push up on his forehead when he pored over a book. He carried his head and shoulders forward in a scholarly stoop.

He took a tie from the rack in the closet. It was already knotted and looped and he was about to put it over his head when she said, "Not that tie. There's a stain on it."

"So I'll keep my jacket buttoned."

"No, you'll forget. Put this one on."

With ill-concealed exasperation, he took the tie she held out to him. Like the first, it was already tied. He put it over his head and pulled the knot up. "Satisfied?" he asked.

"That's much better. You can loosen it now, but be sure to remember to pull it up when you get to the school. Do you have a comb in your jacket pocket?"

"Yes, I have a comb."

"Because driving with the windows down, your hair will be all messed up."

"Any other instructions?" he asked sarcastically.

"Yes. You'll be driving in with your collar unbuttoned and your tie pulled down. So when you get to the school, before you leave your car, button your shirt and pull up your tie. And comb your hair in the rearview mirror. You'll be comfortable once you get inside because it's air-conditioned."

"How do you know it's air-conditioned?"

"They have a Summer Session, so they're bound to have the building air-conditioned. You've got to look right. It's a strange place where you know no one."

"What do you mean, I know no one? I know the president—"

"How many times did you actually see him? Twice? Three times?"

"And I know Roger Fine."

"You haven't seen the Fines since they moved to Newton a couple of years ago."

"And I know that young fellow Jacobs, Mordecai Jacobs, who's engaged to the Lerner girl. And I'll bet there are a bunch of kids from right here in the congregation who go there, and probably some faculty members who live in Barnard's Crossing and have seen me on the street."

She looked at her watch. "What time is your appointment?"

"Two o'clock."

"Then you'd better get started right now. It's half past twelve. How are you going?"

"I thought I'd go by the Boston Road; it's pleasanter."

"But it's fifteen or twenty minutes longer. Better go by the State Road. This time of day, there shouldn't be much traffic."

"All right, I'll take the State Road. And probably have to sit around in his office waiting for him to see me."

"It's better than having him sit around waiting for you."

"It was just by luck," said President Macomber, "that I learned you were available, else I would have got in touch with you sooner. I haven't forgotten the year you were here substituting for Rabbi Lamden." He smiled broadly. He was a handsome man whose face was unlined in spite of his white hair. "As I told you on the phone, we are interested in setting up a Judaic Department, not just having you give the course you gave when you substituted for Rabbi Lamden. That was only a matter of public relations."

"Public relations?"

"That's right. The school was founded in the middle of the last century as a two-year ladies' seminary. And it was called Windermere Ladies' Christian Seminary not because it was in any way denominational or religious—oh, they may have had chapel once a week—but to assure parents that it was a sober, sedate institution and that no high jinks were tolerated. When we became a four-year college and coeducational, albeit largely a fallback school for those who had applied elsewhere and been turned down, we began to attract students from out of state, especially from New York and New Jersey, many of whom were Jews. My predecessor thought it would help matters if we listed a course in Judaic Philosophy and had a rabbi give it. I gather that over the years only Jewish students took it, just as only black students ever register for the course in Black Studies that Reverend Johnson gives. I don't know what the students got out of it other than high marks; A's or at least B's were practically assured."

"Yes, I suspected as much after a couple of sessions," the rabbi said, and then with grim satisfaction, "They quickly realized that I wasn't having it, and that they'd have to work to pass the course."

Macomber nodded. "That's because you were rather old-fashioned in your attitude towards collegiate education: you thought the teacher should teach. By that time the idea had developed that the function of the professor was not to teach, but to engage in research and publish papers in learned journals on his findings. And so his teaching load was cut back to give him more time for research, and if he was prestigious, he did almost no teaching at all. The one or two courses listed in his name in the catalog were apt to be taught by graduate assistants. The college was an ivory tower in which the student profited by being exposed to the atmosphere, I suppose, which is why the students were permitted to take any courses they chose, with no thought that there was a body of knowledge that they had to acquire. Under my predecessor, Windermere went in for that sort of thing; it was the fashion. Still is to a great extent, I suppose. When I came, the Board of Trustees had the same idea, but now I have a board that is inclined to go along with my thinking that teachers should teach and students

6

should learn. And I want our students to have an understanding of how their thinking developed, of the influences that shaped it.

"As a historian I am aware of the importance of Judaic thought in the shaping of Western civilization. During Puritan times it was considered a major influence along with those of Greece and Rome. But after a while Hebrew was dropped from the curriculum, and then Greek and then Latin. Nowadays colleges are more apt to offer a course in Women's Studies or Black Studies. It proves that the institution is modern and free of prejudice. They tend to be snap courses, as is any course given with an ulterior motive, thus ensuring a sizable enrollment. But I want our students to have some understanding of the forces that served to develop our present civilization, and I consider Judaic thought to be one of the major ones."

"You mean it would be a required course?"

"Perhaps in the future," he said cautiously. "Right now, I am planning to develop a core curriculum of what the student should study rather than the free and easy elective system we have now whereby the student can manage to get a degree by taking a number of unrelated courses which he selects because the teacher is reputed an easy marker, or because the course comes at a convenient hour, or—or for whatever reason other than because it is something he should know."

"But what do you want me to do this year?"

"Whatever you think is necessary," Macomber replied promptly. "You might give the same course you gave when you were last here. Or you could start with a seminar for students who have some knowledge of the subject. Or give no course at all for the first semester, but use the time to plan your program. All I ask is that you make yourself available for several hours every day so that you can be consulted by interested students or by faculty, especially from the History and Philosophy departments."

"Once I come in, I'll probably spend most of the day here, except that during the winter months I might want to leave a little earlier to avoid driving after dark."

"You'll be driving in every day?"

"I plan to."

"Well, if you find it taxing, I'm sure you can make arrangements with one of the faculty who live in your town and drive in with him. Let's see, Roger Fine, whom you helped so much when you were last here, I'm sure he'd be glad to give you a lift in every morning."

"The Fines have moved to Newton. And in any case, I wouldn't ask him just because he'd feel obligated."

"Yes, I see what you mean." He thought a moment and then said, "I can get a list of faculty members who live on the North Shore: Barnard's Crossing or Swampscott or Salem, and you could contact them and perhaps arrange with one of them to pick you up."

"Please don't bother. I drove in this afternoon and it was quite pleasant. Of course, if the weather is bad . . ." He shrugged. "I can always take the bus. It stops at my street. It takes a little longer because it goes by way of the Boston Road. Or I could drive over to the Swampscott station and take the train if time is short."

"Well, if you change your mind, let me know." Macomber got up and walked around his desk. He went to the door with the rabbi. "Then we'll expect you here in September."

"I'm looking forward to it," said the rabbi.

Driving back to Barnard's Crossing, he thought of his previous experience at Windermere, of the initial indifference of his class, then their hostility, and finally their enthusiastic acceptance of him. He thought of the peculiar pleasure teaching afforded, the sense of superiority involved in imparting information, and then wondered idly if this was the reason why people enjoyed gossiping.

When he got home Miriam could see that he was pleased and happy and merely asked, "Okay?"

He nodded. "Okay."

Chapter 2

Eʀᴀʀʟy in June, David Small formally resigned from his position of rabbi of the Barnard's Crossing Temple. In his letter of resignation read by the secretary at the regular Sunday morning meeting of the Board of Directors, he mentioned that having served twenty-five years, he was eligible to retire on pension. Except for Al Bergson, the president, with whom he had previously discussed it, the members had had no inkling of his intention, so their reaction was one of bewildered incredulity.

"What's he want to resign for? It's a cushy job with nothing to do except maybe give a little sermon—ten, fifteen minutes—once a week at the Friday evening service."

"He goes to visit the sick at the hospital."

"Big deal! What's he do there? Bless them?"

"And he's in his study practically every day, advising, helping with personal problems."

"These days, you want advice you go to a lawyer, or a doctor, or to a shrink. Let's face it, most of the time he does nothing."

"So maybe he's tired of doing nothing."

"Boy, I'd like a job where I could get tired doing nothing."

"He's going to be teaching," explained Bergson, who was a personal friend of the rabbi. "He'll be professor of Judaic Studies at Windermere College in Boston." Bergson, who ran a travel agency in nearby Salem, was the same age as the rabbi but looked younger because his hair, although thinning, showed no touch of gray. He was a friendly man with a ready smile, and it was hard not to like him.

"Hey, didn't he give a course there a few years back?"

"That's Windermere Christian College. Why would a rabbi want to teach at a Christian college?"

"No longer," said Bergson. "It's just Windermere College of Liberal Arts now. The name was changed this year."

In spite of Bergson's attempts to get them to deal with the other business scheduled for the meeting, they continued to discuss the resignation and its ramifications.

"Look, we'll have to give him some sort of party, won't we?"

"We'll sure as hell have to do something. We can't just say, 'So long, Rabbi. Glad to've met ya.' Not after twenty-five years."

"So what do we do? Have a big dinner?"

"We've also got to give him some sort of gift."

"What sort of gift? We'll be giving him three quarters of his salary year after year. I figure that's a pretty good gift."

"We won't be giving it; the insurance company will."

"I was thinking something like maybe a silver *kiddush* cup with something engraved on it, like, 'From a Grateful Congregation'!"

"How about a set of books?"

"Nah, he's got a roomful of books."

"Look, guys, does it have to be a dinner? How about a luncheon instead?"

"What's the difference?"

"Oh, you know, a luncheon can be light, maybe even dairy foods. A dinner is going to run us a whole lot more."

"So if you're looking to save some money, how's about a brunch?"

"Yeah, that's the ticket; a bagels-and-lox brunch."

"Whatever it is, when would we have it? We can't have it now, in the summer."

"Why not?"

"On account a large portion of the congregation will be going away to their summer places. How do you suppose they'd feel if there's some kind of do and they couldn't take part? The way I see it, we can't have it before September, maybe just before the High Holidays."

"Hey, that's when the new rabbi, the guy we hire to replace Small, will be coming. Right? So we'll have to throw some sort of party for him, won't we? So why don't we plan on combining the two, like a Hail and Farewell party; Hail to the new rabbi and Farewell to the old."

"You know, Ben, you got something there."

"Yeah, that's the ticket, Hail and Farewell."

"But we've got to make some sort of reply to his letter."

"Sure. 'The Board accepts with regret—' "

"With deep regret."

"Yeah, 'With deep regret.' And what do you say, we all sign it? I mean not just the secretary."

"Yeah, that would show him that we're real sorry. So what do we do about getting another rabbi?"

"Oh, the Ritual Committee handles that," said Bergson. "We'd notify the Seminary and—"

"And they'd give us the names of half a dozen young graduates and we'd have to choose one?"

"I think we ought to get someone with experience."

"Oh, I'm sure the Placement Office at the Seminary has the names of quite a few older, experienced men who want to change jobs for one reason or another," said Bergson.

"So what do we do? Tell the Seminary to get in touch with us?"

"Well, I've got to be in New York next week," said Bergson. "I could drop in on them and talk to them about our needs. They would have those who might be interested send us resumes."

"Nowadays, if you're applying for a job, you might have a video made."

"Yeah. They may even have some on file with the Placement Office. If they have, I'll look at them."

"Then what do we do, Al? Have them come here and preach a sermon some Sabbath?"

"Only the finalists," said Bergson.

"The finalists?"

"Sure. The Ritual Committee will check out all who apply. Maybe we'll visit some congregations if they're not too far away. We'll narrow it down to a short list of three or four, and those we'll invite to come here for a Sabbath. My guess is that as soon as our people hear that the rabbi has resigned, we'll have a flood of applicants; relatives, friends of people in our congregation."

"Come to think of it, Al, I've got this uncle in Rhode Island who—"

"So tell him to apply if he's interested."

"What kind of money will we be paying?"

"Same as we've been paying Rabbi Small, I suppose."

"Shouldn't we start the new man lower and let him work up to what we're paying Small? After all, he's been with us for twenty-five years."

Bergson pursed his lips. "I don't think so. The fact is, Rabbi Small's salary is, has been, a little below the standard."

"How come?"

"I suppose because he would never ask for a raise, and he didn't develop a clique who would do it for him," said Bergson quietly.

"Why wouldn't he ask for a raise if he thought he deserved one?"

"And if we turned it down, what would it signify? That we're willing to tolerate him at his present salary, but not at anything more." Bergson shook his head. "No, no, the only way he could ask for a raise would be on an 'or else' basis. 'Give me a raise or I leave.' Just to ask with no indication of leaving if the request is not granted would be begging."

"That's right. A guy asks you for a raise, and you turn him down, you know he's going to begin looking around for another job."

"And it would have been a lot lower if it hadn't been for Howard Magnusson," said Bergson. "When he became president, one of the first things he did was check salaries of temple personnel. As a big business tycoon, he knew you get what you pay for. And when he found the rabbi's salary was low, he forced through a raise."

There was a moment of awkward silence, finally broken by Dr. Ross asking, "So if we're paying below standard, why would anyone want to come to us?"

"Because the guy might be having trouble with his congregation, I suppose," Ben Halprin suggested.

"Or he might have a kid going to one of the colleges around here. He could save himself a lot of money having the kid live at home."

"Fat chance, a kid in college willing to live at home."

"He might just want to live near the ocean."

It was shortly after Miriam had finished with the dishes that the doorbell rang and she opened the door to Police Chief Lanigan, whose friendship with the rabbi and Miriam went back to the year of their arrival in Barnard's Crossing. He was a stocky man with a square face surmounted by a brush of white hair cut so short that the pink of the scalp showed through. "I just happened to be pass-ing," he said, his usual formula when he appeared unexpectedly.

"I hear you're retiring," he said to the rabbi.

"News travels fast," the rabbi remarked dryly.

"It does when you listen for it," said Lanigan. "In a town this size with a small police force, we manage to stay on top of things by keeping our ears open. Sergeant Phelps heard a couple of your members talking about it down at the harbor as they were putting their boat in the water." He sipped at the coffee Miriam had poured for him. "You planning to stay on, or you moving to Boston?"

"To tell the truth, I haven't given the matter any thought," said the rabbi. "It's not easy staying around when you are rabbi emeri-tus. You're a fifth wheel. I suppose that's why so many rabbis go to Israel when they retire. But I like it here, so I expect I'll stay on, at least for a while. I can drive in every day as I used to when I last taught at Windermere."

Lanigan shook his head doubtfully. "That was a few years back," he said. "There's been a pretty sizable increase in traffic since then, and this new tunnel they're building hasn't helped any."

"It's really bad now, David," said Miriam. "I drove in the other day with Edie Bergson and we just inched along. We went by way of the bridge because she said the tunnel was worse. And in the winter when it snows . . ." Her voice trailed off as she thought of the hazard.

"I'll bet you could arrange for a ride in and a ride home every day," said Lanigan. "Quite a few students from here go to Winder-mere, and several members of the faculty live here. There's a Pro-fessor Miller on Evans Road. I could ask him for you."

"Why don't I wait and see how it goes. If the weather is bad, I can always go in by bus."

"The bus goes by the old Boston Road and takes an hour and twenty minutes, and you end up at Haymarket and you've got to take the streetcar from there," Lanigan pointed out.

"Well, I could drive over to Swampscott station and take the train. It's only twenty-three to twenty-five minutes by train," said the rabbi.

"Yes, you could do that," Lanigan admitted. "When is the new rabbi coming?"

"I suppose sometime before the High Holidays. That's right after Labor Day this year."

"How is he chosen? Do you have a chief rabbi who picks one out for you?"

"They have one in England, and in France, and a couple of them in Israel, but we don't have one here in the United States. Here every temple and synagogue is autonomous. It's the Board of Directors through their Ritual Committee who select one from among those who apply or are available. Sometimes they have a likely candidate come down and celebrate a Sabbath so the whole congregation can judge him."

"It seems a funny way to pick a spiritual leader," Lanigan remarked with a shake of the head.

"Ah, but he isn't a spiritual leader," said the rabbi. "Nothing so grandiose. Basically, he's supposed to be sufficiently learned in the law so that he can sit in judgment, although here in America he rarely does. So he does other things: He may be the voice of the congregation in dealing with the rest of the community; he presides at weddings and funerals; he gives sermons during the Sabbath services, following the example of the Christian clergy." He chuckled. "Most of all, in congregations like the one here, he's supposed to be the one practicing Jew."

"Then I'll have to make a point of getting acquainted with this new guy when he comes," said Lanigan.

"I hope it won't be the way you got acquainted with me," said the rabbi, thinking back to his first year when the body of a young woman was found on the temple grounds.

Lanigan grinned sourly.

Chapter 3

IT was after the departmental meeting, at the start of the Summer Session, that Mordecai Jacobs was informed by Professor Sugrue, the head of the English Department, that he had been granted tenure with the accompanying raise in rank from assistant to associate professor. As a result, he felt he could now propose to Clara Lerner.

Later, in the faculty cafeteria, he saw Professor Roger Fine, the other Jewish member of the English Department, and told him the good news. "I suppose Thorvald Miller was also promoted," he added.

Fine shook his head. "Nah, not likely."

"Why not? He came here about the same time I did."

"It used to be that way: if you were hired the third year, you got tenure. Nowadays, it's a matter of scholarship and publication. You've had a couple of papers published—"

"Three."

"All right, three. That's pretty darn good, and they've all been in the *PMLA*, not one of the phony journals that have sprung up in recent years. Besides, your field is Old English, which practically implies scholarship, whereas his field is Modern Literature. People read modern novels and poetry for pleasure. No one is going to read *Beowulf* for pleasure. Thorvald Miller is a nice guy, but they don't grant tenure for niceness."

Curiously, when he told Thorvald Miller about his good fortune, his view was much like that of Roger Fine, and he manifested neither envy of Jacobs nor resentment at having been passed over. "Oh, you were sure to get it, Mord. You're a scholar and they don't want to lose you. Me, I'm just run-of-the-mill. Maybe I'll get tenure in time if I can hang on long enough."

They were friends and worked out together at the gym almost every afternoon when their last classes were over. Jacobs looked scholarly. He was twenty-nine, of medium height, olive-skinned, with dark brown hair surmounting a high forehead. His gray slacks were rarely pressed. One was apt to assume that the suede leather patches on the sleeves of his tweed jacket actually covered holes in the elbows. He was slim and wiry and played a good game of squash.

Miller, thirty-one, was several inches taller, six feet, with a heavy, muscular body. He was blond with a bulging forehead and wide cheekbones. He was always properly dressed. His mother, who lived with him and kept house for him, saw to that. He usually wore suits, and they were always pressed. He wore bow ties and only white shirts, and because he thought they were healthy, white socks. The net effect was that of a farm boy dressed up for a visit to the city.

Although the two had no interests in common other than the college, they usually lunched together, and when Jacobs had made arrangements to see Clara Lerner, his fiancée in Barnard's Crossing, Miller drove him out, dropped him off at her house, and then went on to his own house, which was in another section of the town. He picked Jacobs up the following morning to take him into Boston if he had stayed over.

Although Jacobs had come from a small town in Pennsylvania to study at Harvard, any awe of Cambridge and Boston that he

19

might have had, had long since been dissipated by the time he had taken his doctorate. To him, Boston was merely the city adjoining Cambridge, and he attached no prestige to teaching at Windermere.

He had accepted appointment there in preference to others that had been offered because he thereby had ready access to both the Widener Library at Harvard and the Boston Public Library, as well as because his fiancée lived in Barnard's Crossing and worked in Boston.

To Miller, on the other hand, Boston was still the Athens of America, and the fact that he had obtained a teaching position in a Boston college was a matter of constant self-congratulation. He had come from a small farming town in South Dakota, and had received his doctorate from a state university of no great academic distinction. So he was charmed by this great city with its famous institutions; the world-renowned Boston Symphony, the Mass. General Hospital, the Museum of Fine Arts, as well as the colleges—Harvard, MIT, Boston University, Tufts. He was charmed by the manners, the accent. And by the thought that he was now part of it all.

He had taken a house in Barnard's Crossing in part because he thought the sea air would be good for his mother's asthma, but also because it was on Boston's North Shore with its numerous yacht clubs, where Boston Brahmins had summered since colonial times. Not that he knew any Brahmins, or had ever met one, but he felt the atmosphere was right.

He would have preferred a friend with a name other than Jacobs, but the two got along well together. During the regular school year, both had three-o'clock classes, so both repaired to the gym shortly after four and worked out for an hour or so every day except Wednesdays when Miller had a mysterious engagement elsewhere.

On one occasion, Jacobs asked him, "Where do you go on Wednesday, Thor?"

Miller grinned. "Wednesday, I see a whore lady for a roll in the hay." Then seriously, "You know, Mord, if you're not married and you're teaching in a coed school, you should get your ashes hauled regular, or else you're apt to start fooling around with some coed who flashes a thigh as she crosses her leg, and get into a lot of trouble."

Chapter 4

THE oldest member of the English Department, indeed of the
entire Windermere College faculty, was Malcolm Kent. The official retirement age was sixty-seven, and he was seventy. It was not
because of his scholarship, which was mediocre at best, nor of his
popularity with the faculty or the student body, which was negligible, but because he had married Matilda Clark, now deceased,
who had been the last descendant of Ezra Clark, one of the
founders of the school, who had donated the brownstone front
on Clark Street that had housed the school in its early years. As
the school grew, it acquired one by one the other houses on
Clark Street; all except the brownstone on the corner, which was
the Clark residence where Matilda had lived.

She had willed the building to the college with the proviso that
she and her husband would continue to live there and that the
college would maintain it.

Professor Kent, something of a dandy, wore dark gray suits and
shirts with starched collars. He was well aware of his strategic position as the husband of the late Matilda Clark, and did not hesitate
to presume on it. When he turned sixty-seven and it was suggested to him that he retire, he said, "Then what will I do? No, I'll
stay on for a while."

The matter came up and was discussed at one of the quarterly meetings of the Board of Trustees. Charles Dobson, who had a Cadillac agency in the city, said, "Look, even in today's market the Clark house is worth at least two million dollars. If he got sore at us—"

"What could he do? The house was willed to us."

"Yeah, but he's got dower rights."

"I thought they abolished dower rights in this state."

"He's also got general power of appointment," said George McKittrick, who came down from Bangor, Maine, to attend the meeting. "If he decided to sell it off to somebody, we'd go to court, of course, but my lawyer tells me we'd probably lose."

"He only teaches a couple of courses," said Dobson, "so what harm if he gives them another year or so?"

"Yes, but he hangs around the English office all day," said Nelson Ridgeway.

"So?"

"So he's a pest. Someone comes in to talk to one of the other men in the department, he'll butt into the conversation. I'm sort of friendly with Sugrue, the head of the department, and he told me that once when he wanted to talk to him, he barged into his classroom and interrupted the lecture."

"It's just that he's old and friendless."

In the end, they decided that the desirability of the house far outweighed his nuisance value and voted to let him stay on.

So he stayed on, giving a course in Classics of English Literature, and for the rest of the day reading newspapers and magazines and engaging in idle conversation with anyone who appeared to be free, usually about the important people he had met. Occasionally he would ask someone to get a book for him from the college library, explaining that he could not go himself because he had twisted his ankle and it pained him to go up and down stairs. Most often it was Sarah McBride whom he would ask.

The usual formula was, "Sarah, my love, would you do me a small favor?"

She usually complied because, as she explained to Mordecai Jacobs, "He's a big shot here and since I don't have a Ph.D. and am the latest appointee, I'm the most vulnerable. He's always touching me, on the arm, on the shoulder, when he asks me. He has a class in the room next to mine for my three-o'clock, and he puts his hand around my waist when we go back to the English office. He says it steadies him going down the stairs. I told Lew about it, and he was all for going to see him and telling him to lay off, but I couldn't have that. It might cause all kinds of trouble for me."

Because of his connection with the Clark family, he occasionally received invitations to receptions given by the charities and institutions to which Ezra Clark had formerly contributed, and then for the next few days tell what he had said to the head of the Mass. General Hospital or to the senator who had been the guest speaker.

One day, just before the Fourth of July vacation, in the afternoon, he came in dressed in tuxedo and patent leather pumps, but with the ends of his bow tie hanging loose from his collar. "Does anyone here know how to tie a bow tie?" he asked. "I've got a tendinitis and can't raise my left arm."

"Isn't it just like tying a shoelace?" Jacobs said.

"Why don't you use one of those that hook on?" asked Roger Fine.

"Oh, impossible. I'd be just as apt to wear polyester as a clip-on tie."

Just then, Thorvald Miller entered. Kent's eyes lit up. He pointed at Miller's throat.

"You can tie a bow tie," he said.

"Sure."

"Then will you please tie mine?"

"Sure, turn around."

He turned around, and as Miller reached over his shoulders, Kent murmured, "When my wife used to tie my bow tie, she also had me turn around."

"It's the only way you can do it," said Miller. "There."

Kent felt of the knot at his throat and then went to the small mirror on the wall. "Beautiful," he pronounced. "You must come over to my place and have a drink with me."

"Well, I was going to work out in the gym."

"I insist. Besides, there's something I want to show you."

Miller looked at Jacobs and shrugged. "Okay."

When next Jacobs asked Miller if he was going to the gym, Miller answered, "No, Mord, I'm having tea with Kent." Jacobs got the impression that Miller was prideful at the idea of taking afternoon tea, which he probably regarded as a Boston custom.

At noon the next day when Jacobs suggested they go to the cafeteria for lunch, Miller said, "I'm going with Kent." He then went on to explain, "Look, Mord, Kent is a power here, and I figure the only way I'm going to get tenure is with him behind me."

"I understand, Thor."

Friday afternoons when Jacobs normally went to Barnard's Crossing to spend the weekend with the Lerners, his future in-laws, he could usually count on a ride by Miller, but this Friday Miller told him, "Look, Mord, I won't be able to drive you out this afternoon. Kent is coming out for the weekend, and I'm driving his car."

"Sure, I understand."

"See, this house I'm living in, it turns out that his folks, or his wife's folks, I guess, well, they built it. They owned all the land down there from the old Boston Road to the cove, and he said he'd like to see it again."

From then on, Miller and Kent always seemed to be together. Roger Fine referred to them as the Odd Couple, and the sobriquet caught on. No longer did Kent hang around the English office; he was apt to stay at home, and Miller would join him there when he was free.

Kent spent almost every weekend in Barnard's Crossing with the Millers, and he was frequently invited by Thorvald's mother to come out for dinner on Wednesdays to keep her company until her son got home. On occasion, he took the bus that ran along the old Boston Road, and then walked up the right-of-way to Evans Road and the Miller residence.

At the end of the Summer Session Thorvald Miller was promoted to the rank of associate professor and given tenure.

Chapter 5

THE Ritual Committee worked conscientiously through the summer. They listened to the tape recordings of sermons submitted by candidates for the job. A couple sent in videotapes that, needless to say, showed the candidate in full regalia—black gown, long silk prayer shawl, and a high yarmulke like those worn by cantors. They visited several synagogues so that they could see the candidate on his home ground, and they invited a few, the more likely ones, to come to Barnard's Crossing to celebrate a Sabbath. This consisted of the candidate conducting the Friday evening service, which involved a short sermon, the Saturday morning service, calling for a somewhat longer, more formal sermon, and the Saturday evening or Havdala service. Since there was a collation of tea or coffee and cake provided by the Sisterhood after the Friday service and frequently a *kiddush* with wine and whiskey to wash down herring or smoked fish on crackers after the Saturday morning service, the attendance was fairly large at both and there was plenty of opportunity for the general congregation to meet with the candidate.

The members of the Ritual Committee had been unable to agree on a single candidate, but they had finally arrived at a short list of three, and late in August the Board of Directors met as a committee of the whole to select one. Only about fifteen members of the Board attended regularly, week after week, some of them because they had children in the Sunday School whom they would deliver at nine o'clock and found it more convenient to attend the Board meeting than to go home and have to return for their children at noon. There were others who attended only occasionally. On this Sunday, however, almost all came because they had been notified that the meeting would be for the purpose of selecting a new rabbi.

Al Bergson, the president, rapped for order and said, "All right, let's get the show on the road. I suggest that we dispense with the usual procedure and just spend the time talking rabbi. Any objections?"

"No, let's get on with it."

"Sure, why waste time?"

Similar cries from several others showed that the Board concurred wholeheartedly.

"All right. Now, one or more members of the Ritual Committee checked twenty-three candidates, of which eight were recent seminary graduates. Some of them have had temporary jobs—"

"The rest are rabbis with regular congregations?"

"You mean all those rabbis with jobs want out? What's wrong with them? What's wrong with the job?"

"Are we offering more money than most congregations are?" asked Dr. Marcus.

"As I explained when the subject first came up," said Bergson, "we're on the low side salary-wise. A couple of those who applied would have to take a sizable cut to come here."

"So why—"

"Why would they want to come here? Because we're less than twenty miles from Boston, one of the great cultural centers of the world with the symphony and the museum and all the colleges, and it's also one of the great medical centers of the world."

28

"Point of order." It was Ira Schwarz, a stickler for regulations. Bergson sighed. "Yes, Ira, what's your point of order?"

"Well, looks to me that you're going to give the committee report as the chairman, *ex officio.*"

"And you don't think I should because I'm *ex officio?*"

"Oh, that's all right. But giving a committee report is like—like making a motion. So I think you should hand over the gavel to the vice-president. Then when he recognizes you, you make your report."

"But I don't have a gavel," said Bergson with a smile. "I just rap on the desk with my knuckles. So should I give him my hand to hold while I'm making my report?"

There was general laughter, but Ira Schwarz was obstinate. "You know what I mean. You can run the meeting according to Robert's Rules, or you can operate with no rules at all and anybody can talk anytime he wants to and bring up any subject that comes into his mind, whether it's Old Business or New Business or—or anything at all."

"You're perfectly right, Ira. So I am now asking the vice-president to take the chair. Mr. Chairman, may I give the report of the committee on its work in selecting a new rabbi?"

"You may proceed, Mr. Bergson."

"All right. So as I started to say, we're not far from Boston, and besides, we're on the seashore, which means this is as good a place as any to be in a hot summer, and—"

"Okay, okay," said Dr. Marcus, who was a dentist and so not used to being answered at length. "I get the picture."

"Well," Bergson continued, "we finally came up with a short list of three. One or more members of the committee thought that each of the three was the best of the lot. All three came down here to conduct a Sabbath, so you all had a good look at them. Let's see, first we have Rabbi Alan Joseph from Paterson, New Jersey. Archie favors him. He's—"

"He's the one that used all those big words," said Joe Brickner. "I couldn't understand what he was talking about, something about metempsychosis. I had to look it up in the dictionary when I got home."

"Yeah, my wife thought he was awfully deep," said another. "That's because she didn't know what he was talking about either, all this stuff about Martin Buber and Kierkegaard."

"That's the trouble with us Jews: If we don't understand something, we think it's deep."

"Did you know what he was talking about, Archie?"

"Aw, you guys can't recognize class when you see it," Archie retorted, but he made no attempt to argue the point.

"Attaboy, Archie."

"You tell 'em, Archie."

"All right, boys, let's settle down," said Bergson. "Then there's Rabbi Benjamin Cohen of Temple Beth Emeth in New Britain, Connecticut. He's thirty-eight. He comes from an Orthodox family and has been observant all his life. He was top man in his class at the Seminary and is a real Talmud scholar. His sermon, if you remember, was a regular *drusha*, a dissertation, which is what a rabbi's sermon is supposed to be."

"One of the things that bothers me about Cohen," said Joe Brickner, "is that with the name Cohen, he must be a Kohane, a priest. Right? And as I understand it, they're not supposed to go to a cemetery or be in the presence of a dead body. So what happens when, God forbid, somebody dies? I mean does he do the burial service, or does he have to arrange for a substitute?"

"Oh, his being a Kohane wouldn't interfere with his doing a burial service for us," said Bergson. "It just means that he's not supposed to *duchan* for a year, you know, join with the other priests to bless the congregation at the end of the service. We've abolished the blessing by the priests. Only the Orthodox do that. So it wouldn't affect us."

"What do you mean the priests bless the congregation at the end of the service? You mean all the guys named Cohen get up and bless the congregation?"

"Good Lord! You mean you've never seen the Kohanim performing their ritual duty?" Bob Kahn was incredulous. "Didn't you ever go to *shul,* I mean when you were a kid?"

"We went to Temple Israel in Boston. That's the big Reform temple. What do they do?"

"Yeah, I've never seen it either."

"Yeah, what happens?"

"Well, towards the end of the service," Kahn explained, "and that's a holiday service only, the Kohanim, the priests, that is, the descendants of Aaron, leave the sanctuary and go and have their hands washed by the Levites."

"These priests are guys named Cohen?"

"Or Kahn, or Kane, or Katz, or Kagan, or any other name for that matter, but they're all supposed to be descendants of Aaron."

"And the Levites are guys named Levy?"

"Uh-huh, or Levine, or Segal, or whatever. They are supposed to be of the tribe of Levy. Well, after the Kohanim have their hands washed, they take off their shoes and go up in front of the Ark. Then they cover their heads and their upraised arms with their prayer shawls and turn towards the congregation. And then they pronounce the priestly blessing, repeating it after the cantor one word at a time. 'May the Lord bless you and keep you. May He make His face to shine upon you—' "

"Hey, that's Christian. I've heard that in a church."

"Sure, they took it from us."

"Yeah? You one, Bob?"

"Uh-huh."

"And did you ever, you know, bless the congregation?"

"No, but my old man used to all the time."

"Pious, was he?"

"Not particularly. He ate kosher, of course, because that was what he was used to, but he used to work Saturdays. I remember once somebody asked him why he *duchaned* when he didn't observe the Sabbath, and he said he did it so the rabbi shouldn't."

"I don't get it."

Kahn shrugged, but Bergson sought to explain. "I guess what he meant was that if the Kohanim who are just ordinary members of the congregation didn't do it, then the rabbi might start doing it, and people would get to thinking that he was some sort of holy moly. You know, like a Protestant minister or a Catholic priest, and that's not what he's supposed to be. It's happened in some of the Reform temples and in some of the Conservative ones, too."

"Well, I'm not worried about Rabbi Cohen not going to the cemetery," said Henry Myers, "but we've got to keep in mind the PR aspect. In a small Yankee town like Barnard's Crossing, the PR aspect of the rabbi can be very important.

"That was a pretty good sermon he gave the Friday night he was here, but I couldn't help thinking that Rabbi Cohen was not too prepossessing physically. He's short and fat and bald and he seemed to be sweating a lot."

"Yeah, I noticed that. His head was glistening. It bothered me, too. On the other hand, Rabbi Dana Selig—now, he makes a real good impression. He's tall and he's what my daughter calls 'a hunk.' What's more, according to his resume, he played football when he was in college. Believe me, that won't hurt us with the Gentiles."

"Joe and Ira favored him," Bergson admitted. "And I guess he made a good impression when he came to do a Sabbath for us, but he doesn't have much of a background."

"What's that supposed to mean? He graduated from the Seminary, didn't he?"

"Sure, but his folks are Reform and nonpracticing at that, so all he knows is what he got at the Seminary. I mean, it isn't as though he grew up in it." He looked around the room for some indication of understanding. There was no response, so he went on, "And we've also got to take into consideration his wife."

That did evoke a response. "What's the matter with his wife? She's a very attractive woman."

"Well, when he was first interviewed by the committee, he made it plain that his wife was no part of the deal; that we were not to expect her to play the part of the traditional rebbetzin because she had her own interests."

"She's a lawyer, isn't she?" asked Dr. Marcus.

"That's right."

"Well, look, you've got to expect that these days," said Marcus. "I mean all the women are apt to have interests different from their husbands. My wife is an architect, for instance. Maybe thirty, forty years ago when the professions weren't open to them, their interests were the same as their husbands'. So my Sybil would have been the receptionist in my office, or maybe she'd have taken some courses and become my dental hygienist. But these days . . ." He raised his shoulders and then let them drop in resignation.

As the discussion continued, it was evident that the majority by far favored Rabbi Selig. The desultory criticism continued, however; it was normal at Board meetings. One objected that Rabbi Selig had a beard.

"But he keeps it trimmed. It's not a hippie beard. Strictly speaking, a rabbi is supposed to have a beard."

Another raised the question of his name. "What kind of name is Dana? Is this a name for a rabbi?"

"His Hebrew name is Daniel," said Bergson. "I mean that's the name we'd use if he were called up to read a portion of the Torah."

"Sure, Dana is just an American name like—er—Kevin or Hilary."

"Did you get a look at his socks when he was sitting up on the bimah?"

"And that tie was pretty wild; for a rabbi, I mean."

However, when the clock on the wall showed noon, their regular time of adjournment, Bergson rapped for order and said, "Okay, guys, let's put it to a vote."

Chapter 6

THE Hail and Farewell Dinner, which had been reduced to a lunch, and was finally downgraded to a bagels-and-lox brunch, turned out to be a lot more Hail than Farewell. A few came up to Rabbi Small to say they were sorry he was leaving and to wish him well in his new job. And a few came to talk to him about Windermere because they had a son or a daughter who had gone there, or was now attending, or had applied for admission. But as was only to be expected, most of the attention was directed to the new rabbi, a tall, handsome man with a carefully trimmed mustache and a short beard that covered only his chin.

The two rabbis had little chance to talk to each other. However, Rabbi Selig did manage to say that he and his wife would like to come to the Smalls' some afternoon to pay their respects, and Rabbi Small had said that any afternoon would do. "Have Mrs. Selig arrange it with Mrs. Small. But why not come to dinner some evening instead?"

They came to dinner a few days later. They had been living in a hotel in nearby Salem while looking for a more suitable residence, so Miriam asked, "Have you found a place yet?"

Rabbi Selig grinned broadly. "We're signing a lease for a year tomorrow, with an option to buy. It's furnished, but they'll move all their stuff out if we decide to buy. There's a lot of land, over an acre, we were told."

"Mowing a lawn that size can be quite a chore," Rabbi Small observed.

Selig laughed. "Not this lawn; it's all rock. Oh, there are small patches of earth here and there with low bushes or some grass. He's got one of those old-fashioned hand lawn mowers for the grassy bits. See, it's right near the coast—you can see the ocean from our windows in the back—and except for a few yards of sandy beach, the whole area is rock. The road to Boston runs by the front of the house. In fact, there's a bus stop right at the driveway that leads up to the house, which I figure could be handy if I wanted to go into Boston and not have to worry about finding a place to park. The driveway is pretty steep. See, we're on a level patch on a hill, and the driveway ends up as a sort of ter-race on the side where the entrance to the garage is. It's all as-phalt and I'll have to keep it clear during the winter, I suppose, because driving up that hill might be tough if there's snow on the ground. But he's got a snowblower, so it shouldn't take long to clear it."

"Dana can't wait for it to snow so he can try it out," his wife re-marked fondly.

Rabbi Selig grinned. "Yeah, I do like to fool around with tools and machines."

"Oh, I think I know where the house is," said Miriam. "It's right at the boundary between Barnard's Crossing and Swamp-scott. There's a sign there saying that you're now entering Barnard's Crossing."

"That's right," said Selig. "It's just beyond our driveway, com-ing from Boston, but we're in Barnard's Crossing. I was told that the sign was put up beyond our driveway because our side is all rock. It was easier to put up the sign beyond us rather than on the actual boundary, where they would have had to blast. See, it's not the regular Highway Department sign; it's a billboard put up by the chamber of commerce which tells when the town was founded and then goes on to say that it's the birthplace of the American navy."

"And there's a hedge running along the side, isn't there?" Miriam asked.

"That's right. And there's an electric hedge trimmer to take care of it. Which means what? An hour or two once a week during the summer."

"The hedge, that's the boundary of the property?" asked Miriam.

"It actually extends a few feet beyond the hedge. Beyond that, the land is level and grassy, which means there is a drop of about twelve feet, almost vertical, opposite the house, which is why the hedge was planted in the first place, I suppose. This terrace by the side of the house has a badminton net strung across it. So I imagine if you ran back after a birdie, you could sustain a nasty fall."

Susan Selig, a tall brunette of thirty-four, with hair gathered in a bun at the nape of the neck, was a couple of years older than her husband. When they finished eating, she insisted on helping Miriam with the dishes, and then remained in the kitchen with her so that they could talk more freely than they might in the presence of the men. In the living room the men settled back in their armchairs.

"You know, I think I'm going to like this congregation," said Selig.

"Didn't you like the one you left?"

"Oh, I liked it well enough, but I wasn't really comfortable there. They were an older congregation and . . ." He hesitated, and then in a more earnest tone, went on, "See, Rabbi, there's a difference between knowing something by studying it, and knowing it because you've grown up in it. My folks weren't the

least bit religious. I mean, they never went to a temple or a synagogue, not even on the High Holidays. And I didn't even attend a Sunday School. I took a course in the History of Religion
in my senior year in college because—because it was supposed
to be a snap course. And it was, but I got terribly interested in
Judaism as a result. And when I graduated I applied for admission to the Seminary. It took me seven years to get my degree
there, but in dealing with my congregation I still felt like someone who has taken a Berlitz course talking to a native. See what
I mean?"

"And here?"

"Well, this congregation is a lot younger, and I get the feeling
that a lot of them have the same background I have. At least,
that's the feeling I got when I met with the Board of Directors."

"Really? From what was said, or—"

Selig laughed shortly. "More from the way they reacted to what
I said. Like, I jog two or three times a week. Well, my old congregation, at least many of the members, were pretty upset if they saw
me in shorts or a sweat suit. I mentioned to the Board here that I
jog and a couple of them said they did, too, and maybe we could
run together."

"That would be Bob Kruger and Henry Myers, I imagine," said
Rabbi Small.

"I wouldn't know. I was introduced to all of them, of course,
but I don't remember all of the names. Well, that was just one
thing. There were other little hints that I got that suggested this
was a different kind of congregation from my old one. When I
was first contacted, for instance, I told them that if they hired me,
that's all they'd get; that my wife would not be part of the deal. I
mean she wouldn't be the traditional rebbetzin, going to all the
Sisterhood and Hadassah meetings. She has her own career.
She's a lawyer. It was the cause of some flak in my former con-

gregation, but these guys just nodded, like it was only to be expected."

"Will she be practicing here?" asked Rabbi Small. "Has she made arrangements with some local law office?"

"Not yet. See, she has to pass the Mass. bar exam in order to practice here. She's planning to take a bar review this year to prepare for it."

"Well, I wish her luck."

Later, after the Seligs had gone, Miriam asked, "What do you think of him, David?"

"I think he'll be popular with the congregation. He's just what they want. He's tall and good-looking, so the women will like him. And he's young, so the younger men who constitute the majority will feel he's one of them. Yes, he should do all right here. Probably a lot better than I did."

A few days later, when the two rabbis met at the minyan, Rabbi Small asked, "Well, how do you like your new house?"

"It's fine. Yesterday, when it was so hot, we sat on the verandah, and it was delightfully cool. Oh, a funny thing happened. While we were sitting on the verandah, a man came walking up the driveway. I thought he was coming to see me, but he walked right on. So I hailed him, and when he didn't answer, I called out, 'You're trespassing.' Without even stopping, he shouted back, 'Right-of-way,' and went right on. So I called the agent that rented us the place and he said there might be a right-of-way to the beach; that he'd look it up."

"It bothers you?"

"Well, if there is a right-of-way to the beach, not too many will be making use of it with the summer practically over. But I don't think I'd care to buy a place where people could come traipsing along with their kids and hampers and beach umbrellas."

"That could be annoying, especially if you happen to be having a party outdoors. Your agent thinks there might be a reference to a right-of-way in a previous deed?"

"I guess so, but my wife says that if it's a right-of-way that has always been exercised, there might be no mention of it in any deed."

"I could ask Hugh Lanigan. He'd know if anyone would."

"Hugh Lanigan? Who's he?"

"He's the chief of police and he's lived here all his life."

"Gee, I'd appreciate it if you could find out definitely one way or another."

"I'll make a point of it."

❖   ❖   ❖

And because it occurred to Rabbi Small that if there was a legal right-of-way, it would certainly be likely to be used on a Saturday, and Rabbi Selig's Sabbath might be disturbed as a result, he made a point of taking a trip downtown to see Lanigan and ask about it.

"That's the old Clark estate," said Lanigan. "Ezra Clark was a big-shot realtor in Boston. He bought the land from the old Boston Road all the way to Gardner's Cove on the ocean. Got it dirt cheap, too, because it was mostly ledge. He built a house on what is now Evans Road. It's now occupied by a man named Miller, Professor Miller, I think. He teaches at your school and he was one of those I was going to ask about a ride for you. There was no street there at the time, but Clark chose that spot because there is some soil there so he could have a lawn. Then when his kids were grown and were having their friends come out, he put up another house on the top of the hill, the one your rabbi is in. Both houses were just summer shacks, but after the town put the street in, Evans Road, that is, he winterized them because he planned to sell them, I guess. See, the kids were grown now, and

traveling—to Europe and elsewhere summers—and weren't using the place much. Well, of course, he still thought of it as one
parcel of land even though one of the houses was now on Evans
Road and the other on the old Boston Road. And he'd just walk
across the land that was now part of the house on the hill if he
wanted to take the bus in to Boston, or if he came from Boston.
And the kids and their friends would walk across his land when
they wanted to go down to the beach. When he sold one of the
houses—to a fellow named Willoughby—it was assumed that he'd
have access to the beach. So Willoughby gave him access to the
bus stop at the foot of the driveway. And though both properties
have changed hands a couple of times, it's been that way ever
since."

On his way downtown, the rabbi had circled to get a look at
Rabbi Selig's house, so now he asked, "That hedge that runs
alongside the driveway, that's the boundary of Rabbi Selig's
lot?"

"No, it runs about three feet beyond the hedge, right to where
the ledge drops off. By a sort of general agreement, it's that three-
or four-foot strip that has become the right-of-way. That's not why
the hedge was put up, though. It was put up because one of the
Willoughby kids, while playing, roller-skating, I think, on that as-
phalt terrace at the end of the driveway, took a tumble off the
ledge. Broke his leg, I remember. And that level land beyond
the ledge, that was part of the property originally, but it was too
narrow—it comes down to a point between Evans Road and the
curve of the Boston Road—to build on, according to the zoning
code, I mean. So Willoughby ceded it to the town, which cut his
taxes a little and also put the burden of maintaining it on the
town, cutting the grass and planting a few flowers, that sort of
thing. But if your rabbi is worried about kids with sand pails and
umbrellas traipsing across his land to the beach, tell him to forget

it. It leads to Gardner's Cove, which is more pebbles than sand and is apt to be pretty much covered with seaweed most of the time."

"I'm sure he'll be glad to hear it. He was quite concerned."

"And you were concerned for him?"

"Him and the congregation. The last thing they need is for their rabbi to get into a hassle with their neighbors."

Chapter 7

Rabbi Selig had driven around the town not only to acquaint himself with the location of the various buildings that might prove important to him—the town hall, the post office, the library, and the various churches—but also the route he might take for his morning jog. This last he had gone over very carefully, checking to see that it was fairly level all the way, but also to make sure that it did not involve heavily trafficked streets where he might be recognized and greeted and perhaps have to stop to talk. The route he finally decided on ran for two miles on a street that followed the shoreline to the public wharf. For a good part of the way, it ran parallel to Abbot Road, the main street, and was connected to it at several points by intersecting streets.

Monday morning, he tested it. He drove to what he decided would henceforth be his starting point, a couple of hundred yards beyond his driveway, parked his car, and began jogging easily with the intention of gradually increasing his pace. The total run, back and forth, would be just four miles as measured on the odometer of his car and would constitute what he thought would be a good workout for the day.

The weather was warm but with a slight breeze off the ocean, which kept him relatively cool. At one point he passed a large estate fenced in with a shoulder-high iron railing behind which a small white terrier barked at him as he approached and then ran alongside yapping hysterically until he passed the end of the fence.

When he finally reached the wharf, his turning point, he was perspiring nicely and reluctant to stop for fear of cooling off. But there was a lobster boat that had just docked, and he could not help watching as the catch was being unloaded.

A voice behind him said, "Maybe another drop in the price of lobster at the local restaurants."

He turned, and saw a man of approximately his own age similarly dressed in jogging togs. He was tall, with shrewd eyes and a pointed chin and dark hair. The rabbi didn't want to start a conversation, but out of simple politeness he felt he had to answer. "That's a large catch, is it?"

"It sure is. Look how many in each trap. Of course, some of them are too small and will have to be thrown back in the water, but there are lots of big ones, and that makes for lower prices in the fish markets and the restaurants. But I don't suppose that would interest you particularly. You're the new rabbi, aren't you? Someone pointed you out the other day."

Rabbi Selig nodded. "That's right, and no, the price of lobster doesn't concern me."

"Well, me, I generally keep to kosher food because my folks were observant. No pork products, no butter on my bread when I'm having meat because, well, you know, your stomach can't help reflecting its early training even when you've outgrown the reasons for it. But somewhere along the line, I acquired a taste for lobster and I like it once in a while, but only when I eat out."

"Are you a member of my congregation, Mr.—er—?"

"Baumgold," the other said, and held out his hand.

They shook hands. "No, I'm not a member of any temple or synagogue. My folks were members of the place in Salem and I went to the Religious School there when I was a youngster, but I resented having to go after school when all the other kids were on the street playing. I stood it until my Bar Mitzvah and then I dropped the whole business entirely." He chuckled. "My wife is not Jewish, but she's a lot more interested in it than I am. She teaches at Windermere College in Boston and she's planning to audit a course in Judaism there. Come to think of it, it's your predecessor here who'll be giving it." He chuckled again. "Maybe she'll convert me."

Rabbi Selig managed a smile. "Stranger things have happened," he said, and then, "I've got to be getting back."

"Which way do you go? Ocean Street? I could run with you part of the way. I cut off at Endicott."

Rabbi Selig jogged every day that the weather permitted. He would start out a little after six, get home usually by a quarter to seven, shower, and drive to the temple in time for the morning service. The service lasted only about twenty minutes, so that even when he stopped to talk to one of his congregants, he was back at home by half past seven when he would have his breakfast.

More often than not, Baumgold would join him at Endicott Street and the two would run side by side to the wharf. There they would stop for a minute or two, ostensibly to remove a pebble from a shoe or to retie a lace or just to stare out at the harbor; Selig, more zealous, usually jogged in place. But they always managed to talk before starting back. On learning that Baumgold was a lawyer with an office in Salem, the rabbi remarked that his wife was also a lawyer.

"That so? With some local firm, or a Boston outfit?"

"She was with a large firm in Connecticut, but she has to pass the Massachusetts bar exam first before she can practice here," said Rabbi Selig. "She is planning to take a bar review."

"Oh yeah? She signed up for one yet? Because a fellow I know gives one right here in Salem. And he's good. He gives them right in his house and he only takes about a dozen at a time. If she's interested—"

"I'll mention it to her."

He did mention it to his wife, and she said, "It's an idea. I've been asking around, and everyone said I'd have to go in to Boston. If I could get one in Salem, it would be a lot easier. Why don't you ask him to drop by so I could ask him about it? I'd also like to ask him about this trespasser and the right-of-way business."

"Okay, next time I see him. But look here, it's a legal matter, isn't it? Couldn't you—"

"Oh, I know the law in general. It's the local practice I'm concerned with. It could be that the law is against it, but that it is common practice to ignore it. And if we go against the common practice on the ground that there is a law against it, we might get in bad with the locals, and that wouldn't be good for us, or for the congregation either."

Chapter 8

RABBI Selig was somewhat surprised to find that he had to tell Baumgold how to get to his house when he invited him to drop over for coffee some afternoon. "It's on the Boston Road," he explained, "right where Barnard's Crossing adjoins Swampscott."

"Oh, well, I hardly ever get up around there. I take the new State Road when I go to and from Boston."

"The Boston bus uses our road," Selig pointed out. "There's a stop right at our driveway."

"Probably to avoid traffic and traffic lights," said Baumgold.

"Well, anyway, you can't miss it. There's a biggish sign just beyond our land that says, 'Welcome to Barnard's Crossing.' "

"So if it's beyond your property, you're actually a resident of Swampscott rather than Barnard's Crossing."

"No, we're in Barnard's Crossing. I guess they put the sign up beyond us because there's earth that they could drive a couple of stakes into. If they were to put it on the other side of our driveway, they'd have to either blast or drill. It's all ledge. Our house is on a hill and most of it is ledge. There are patches of soil here and there, so we have some grass, but mostly it's ledge."

"So why in the world did someone think to build a house there?"

"For the bathing, I suppose. There's this small bay—"

"Gardner Cove, right? I've jogged along the shore a couple of times."

"That's right."

"Now I know where you are. But I thought those were all summer cottages up around there."

"I guess they were," said Selig, "but the present owner, the man we're renting from, said that our place has been thoroughly winterized. On the couple of cold days we've had, it's been quite comfortable."

It was a pleasant, sunny day when Baumgold drove up to the Selig home. Rabbi Selig heard him and came out to greet him. The two stood outside as Baumgold looked around. "Your land goes up to the hedge?" he asked.

"And a couple of feet beyond," said Selig. "There's a twelve-foot drop there, so I suppose the hedge was put up to keep anyone from falling over in the dark. As I understand it, the man that built this house originally owned all the land from the Boston Road to the beach, including the flat land beyond the drop. And he built not only this house, but that one across the road there. Do you see it? For a married son or daughter, I understand. I guess this place wasn't big enough for them, his kids, and their friends. Of course, there was no road dividing the two houses then. That came later."

"Cutting you off from the beach, huh?"

"Well, no. At least I don't think so," said Selig. "The man we're renting from said we had a right-of-way. Say we do; does that mean that the people from that other cottage have a right-of-way through our property, to the bus stop, I mean?"

"Gosh, I wouldn't think so. It all depends on what is written into the deed. You'd have to look it up in the Registry. Have they been coming through your property?"

"Well, not really. But the other day someone came up along the hedge, not on the outside, you understand, but on this side of it. He was visiting the people in that other cottage, I suppose. I hailed him and when he didn't answer, I shouted out that he was trespassing. And without bothering to halt in his stride, he yelled back, 'Right-of-way,' and walked on."

Baumgold shrugged. "What can I tell you? But you're renting only for a year, right?"

"Yeah, but we might buy. The owner was a lot more interested in selling than in renting. It's very pleasant and nicely situated. We can see the ocean from our bedroom windows. And being right at the bus stop on the Boston Road could come in handy, especially if Susan has to go into Boston for her bar review. I mean, it might be easier to take the bus than to drive in and try to find a place to park."

"Yeah, that's for sure. But if she were to take this bar review in Salem—"

"That's what she wants to ask you about. Let's go in through the back by way of the garage."

Selig led him through the open door of the spacious two-car garage. Inside, Baumgold nodded appreciatively. He pointed to the workbench against the far wall and the Peg-Board above it from which dangled a few tools.

"Your tools?" he asked.

"No, they come with the house. My own are back in Connecticut in storage with my furniture."

"And the snowblower in the corner there?"

"That also comes with the house."

"You might need that if we have a snowy winter. You might have trouble getting up your driveway even with snow cords. That's a pretty steep hill you've got there."

"I know. It occurred to me when we were first shown the place, but the owner said that with the snowblower I could clear the driveway in fifteen or twenty minutes."

This last as they entered the kitchen where Susan Selig was setting cake and cookies on a plate and arranging cups and saucers on a tray. "And he's dying to try it out," she said gaily. "Why don't you guys go into the living room and I'll bring in the coffee."

"Why don't we have our coffee here," the rabbi suggested.

"All right."

So they sat at the kitchen table as Baumgold explained about the bar review in Salem. "He holds the class right in his home. See, his wife is not well. I don't know what's the matter with her, but she wants him there all the time. So he had to practically give up his law practice. But he's a born teacher, and those who have taken his review swear by him. He keeps it sort of informal, like when they finish a section, say torts, or contracts, or jurisprudence, or whatever, they have like a kaffeeklatsch, in his home, or in the home of one of the students."

"Sounds interesting," said Mrs. Selig.

"If you like, I'll give him your name and he'll send you some literature, or call you."

"You do that. I have a flyer from a school in Boston, but I'll hold off until I hear from him."

Chapter 9

THE faculty meeting on Monday, the day before registration, was called for eleven. Because the announcement said "All members of the faculty are strongly urged to attend," the rabbi sensed that attendance was not actually required. However, there was a penned note at the bottom that read, "Can you manage to see me before the meeting? Anytime after ten will do." It was signed by Dr. Cardleigh, the dean of the college.

It occurred to the rabbi that if he started out a little before nine, he would miss the morning traffic and still be in good time for his meeting with the dean. He chose to go by way of the old Boston Road, which followed the curvature of the coastline. He noted with satisfaction that he was able to reach the college a little before ten, and since school had not yet begun, he had no trouble finding a place to park.

Dr. Cardleigh was a big man, tall with broad shoulders, but he seemed to be trying to make himself small by the way he slouched in his chair. He twisted about as though to get comfortable and finally came to rest on the back of his spine with one leg dangling over the arm of his chair, exposing an unpressed trouser leg and a scuffed and dusty shoe.

His high forehead was surmounted with sparse, graying hair,

and although clean-shaven, his cheekbones, which were prominent, showed some fuzz, which he had evidently not bothered to reach with his razor. His large upper lip was covered by a straggly mustache beneath a bulbous nose. Evidently he was not a man concerned about his appearance, and for some reason the rabbi felt comfortable with him.

"I was on sabbatical the year you were here, Rabbi," he said, "but I heard all about you from President Macomber and some others when I got back. I was offered the deanship after the—er—departure of Dean Hanbury." He chuckled. "It was just as well, I suppose, because I had about run out of students. I had been in the Classics Department, you see, and my last year of teaching I had only two students in Latin and none in Greek. I took the sabbatical because the following year, when you came, no one signed up for any of my courses."

"You did research that year?"

"No, I just traveled a bit. When I came back, I gave a course in Greek Literature, to English majors mostly. Nevertheless, I was kept pretty busy. It was a bad winter that year, and faculty people kept coming to me with cases of bad colds and flu—" In response to the rabbi's questioning look, he explained, "My doctorate is in medicine. I'm an M.D., not a Ph.D."

"You mean you still practice?"

"Oh no. Don't care for it. I studied medicine under family pressure. My father was a doctor and my grandfather before him, so nothing would do but I should become one, too."

He took a pipe from his pocket and filled it from a pouch that he drew from a desk drawer. He struck a match. "Smoke bother you, Rabbi?" he asked as he puffed away.

"No, I used to smoke a pipe myself," said the rabbi, "but I had to give it up."

"Advice of your doctor?"

"No, it was just that I found it hard to smoke during the week and not be able to on the Sabbath. Lighting a match is making fire, and that is considered work and hence forbidden on the Sabbath. But I'm a little surprised that you do."

"Why?"

"Well, your profession, the medical profession—"

"The medical profession occasionally goes on a crusade, and the most extreme views are apt to prevail. There's also the Puritanism we Americans are prone to. You know, it was said that the Puritans disapproved of bearbaiting, not because it was cruel to the bear, but because it gave pleasure to the spectators. Well, the medical fraternity is the same. They tell us to avoid sugar and fat and salt, anything that makes food taste good. We don't eat meals anymore; we ingest chemicals: potassium and zinc and iron. We don't drink milk or eat cheese; we increase our calcium intake.

"Smoking is taboo because it causes a whole variety of ailments. I suppose cigarette smoking *is* bad for you because you tend to inhale the smoke, but you don't inhale when you smoke a pipe, so they've come up with the notion that it's bad because it makes others, nonsmokers, sick if they're in the same room.

"But there's something in the human psyche that demands some form of—of relaxing, some pleasurable vice. Every society we know about has one. I suppose it's because our minds work all the time, and if we didn't interrupt this constant stream of mentation, we'd all go mad. If you stop one form of relaxing vice, you only break into another."

"So stopping smoking has led to—"

"To drugs and sex," Cardleigh replied promptly. "Drugs and sex and violence, and—and jogging, and lifting weights, and working out at those crazy machines."

He sat up straight in his chair and said, "Well, let's get down to business, Rabbi. I understand you're heading up a new department, but all I have is the course in Judaic Thought that Rabbi Lamden gave until he retired. That was the course you taught the year you substituted for him. Right? I barely had time to change his name for yours in the catalog before going to the printer. Now, is there more? Are you planning other courses?"

The rabbi nodded. "Eventually. But I thought I'd wait until I had a chance to gauge the response of the student body and the faculty, too. Perhaps next year I might have an advanced course for students who have some background in the field."

"Well, I'm concerned right now with the allotment of space, office space and classroom space." From his top drawer he drew a large chart and laid it on top of the desk. "Let's see, your course is three hours a week, Monday, Wednesday, and Friday."

"That's right. At eleven o'clock if possible."

"No trouble with the hour. You have any idea how many you'll draw?"

The rabbi shrugged. "I have no way of knowing."

"I gather from what President Macomber said that you agreed to stick around a few hours every day so that you'd be available to any student or faculty member who might want to consult with you. So you'd need a decent-sized office. We can't have you cooped up in a cubbyhole for three or four hours every day. Now, the Freshman English people are moving in with the rest of the English Department on the second floor here in this building. That leaves their office here on the first floor vacant. It's pretty big as offices go. And if you only get ten or a dozen for your class, you could hold it there instead of in one of the classrooms. I could have some chairs and a blackboard brought in and take out the extra desks that are there now and maybe give you a large table so you could run your class like a seminar. Of course, if you should draw a lot more, we can always find you an empty lecture hall."

"I'd need a bookcase."

"There's one there. If it's not adequate, let me know and I'm sure I can scare up another one." He cocked an inquisitive eye at his visitor. "You'll be doing research, I suppose."

"I wasn't planning to. If you're thinking of the kind of research that's involved in piecing together scraps of parchment of the Dead Sea Scrolls, I'm afraid it's not the kind of thing I do. I have written some papers that have appeared in journals, but they were essentially works of criticism rather than research."

Dr. Cardleigh nodded. "Did you discuss this with Macomber?"

The rabbi shook his head. "The subject didn't come up."

"Ah, he probably knew your attitude from when you were last here."

"What attitude? I don't understand."

Cardleigh leaned back in his chair and in reminiscent tones began, "It used to be that college was a place where the faculty was engaged primarily, I might say solely, in teaching. In their spare time, they did what other people did in their spare time. Occasionally one might get caught up in some interesting problem in his field and work at that. And if it seemed worthwhile, he might write it up and send it on to a learned journal for the benefit of those who might be interested.

"But sometime in the twenties, a change developed. If a professor had discovered something new, or developed a theory that attracted the attention of the press, then Kibosh was no longer Kibosh College of Liberal Arts, but Kibosh Where That Fellow Discovered the New Planet, or the Cure of Cancer. And suddenly everyone connected with the school took on a new importance.

"The administrators soon realized that the power and the prestige, and the endowments and grants, too, came not from teaching, but from research, with the result that appointment to a college faculty was not on the basis of the ability or even the desire to transmit one's knowledge to the student, but rather on one's capacity for research as proved by the articles one had published in learned journals. 'Publish or perish.'

"It wouldn't be so bad if the research resulted in finding something worth knowing. But when you do research because you have to, you end up only with something that can be published in a learned journal—and the number of those has increased enormously—which no one will read. Like Ph.D. dissertations, they have to be original, and that means in the humanities, at least, these days you have to write about people or things that generations of scholars before you didn't consider worth writing about. All the important, worthwhile subjects had already been covered. Imagine spending two, three years, or more, of your life working on the life and writings of some poetaster who managed to get a slim volume of poetry published because his father-in-law was in the printing business." He shook his head in disbelief as he sucked on his pipe.

"Ever hear of Simeon Suggs?" he asked, sitting up straight and removing his pipe from his mouth.

"Simeon Suggs?" asked the rabbi politely. "No, I can't say that I have."

"Neither had I," said Cardleigh, "and I always thought I had a pretty good knowledge of English literature. Well, one of our people wrote his doctoral dissertation on him."

He puffed at his pipe but drew no smoke. "Gone out," he said. "One thing about a pipe: You can't talk and keep it lit. Maybe that's one of the benefits of smoking a pipe. If it were required of our congressmen, we might have a more efficient government. Well, have a good year, Rabbi, and if you need anything, come and see me."

He glanced at his watch and said, "Why, it's almost eleven. You were planning on coming to the faculty meeting, weren't you? Come along then." He extricated himself from behind his desk and came around to the rabbi, who had risen. Putting his arm across his shoulder, he propelled him to the door.

❖　❖　❖

The meeting was being held in a large hall on the first floor. It was immediately apparent to the rabbi that not all the faculty were there. He looked around for someone he might know; one or two looked vaguely familiar, but they showed no sign of recognition when they saw him, so he did not approach them, reflecting that they were probably people he had seen in the corridors, or perhaps in the faculty cafeteria when he had gone there for an occasional cup of coffee when he was last at Windermere years ago. He looked around for Roger Fine, the one faculty member he did know, but Fine evidently had decided not to attend.

Although some were seated, most were standing around in small groups, chatting about how they had spent the summer, or of conferences they had attended. When Dr. Cardleigh ascended the platform at the end of the hall, many of those standing took seats. He came forward to the lectern in front of the platform and said, "All right, ladies and gentlemen, please take seats so we can proceed. I asked to have a copy of the catalog placed on each seat, but I've got a pile up here if any of you missed out on one. The new catalogs won't be delivered for at least a week, I understand, so it's important with registration tomorrow that you be informed of the changes that have been made. If you'll turn to page eleven, you will note that Freshman English is no longer required of all freshmen. Those with a B or better average in English in their senior year in high school are exempt."

"But can they take it if they want to?"

"Yes."

"For credit?"

"Certainly. Any more—er—questions?"

The rabbi sensed that he had almost said "foolish questions." A white-haired man sitting in the first row rose and held up his hand.

"Yes, Professor Kent?"

"I think, Dr. Cardleigh, that because this change is so radical a departure from collegiate tradition and practice, the rationale for it should be explained. I am prepared at this time—"

"Yes, yes, Professor, but I'm afraid we don't have time for it right now," said Cardleigh. "Not if we are planning to have lunch at the usual time. Anyone who objects to the change can see Professor Kent, or the head of the department, Professor Sugrue, and discuss it with him."

"Very well," said Kent stiffly.

There was a chuckle or two, and someone behind the rabbi whispered to his neighbor, "Cardleigh is the only one who stands up to him."

"Now if you'll turn to page fifteen," the dean went on, "please note that Professor Haynes will be on sabbatical this year. His course will be taught by Professor Blanchard."

It went on until they had worked their way through the entire catalog. Then Cardleigh read a list of those who had been dropped, which included two instructors who had taught Freshman English and who were no longer needed since the course was no longer required.

Then Cardleigh announced the new members of the faculty, and each in turn rose and received a scattering of applause. When it came Rabbi Small's turn, Cardleigh said, "Rabbi Small taught here a few years ago. He is now back to head up the new Department of Judaica. This semester he will give one course in Judaic Philosophy, which comes Mondays, Wednesdays, and Fridays at eleven. He will also be in his office, the former Freshman English office, for several hours every day for those who might wish to consult him. A word of warning to student advisers who have to approve student programs: Rabbi Small's course will not be a snap course. As he demonstrated when he was last here, students in his course are expected to work, and to work hard."

The meeting adjourned shortly afterward and all trooped out to go to the cafeteria. The rabbi, however, chose to go home since he was certain there would be little there that he could eat. This time he used the State Road and it took him just an hour. He decided that henceforth he would use the old Boston Road even though it took longer. It was a pleasanter drive and traffic was far less.

Chapter 10

WEDNESDAY morning found Rabbi Small on the platform of the Swampscott train station, ready to board the 8:02 train to Boston's North station, where he would take the subway to Windermere for his first day of teaching. True, his class was scheduled for eleven o'clock, but on this the first day, he felt it was somehow only proper to arrive at the start of the school day.

On the few occasions when he had gone into Boston by train, he had gone either late in the morning or early in the afternoon; never during the rush hour. So he was surprised at the crowd on the platform, and when the train pulled in, he was even more surprised to find that all seats had already been taken—most had got on at Salem, the previous stop—and that he would have to stand. When the train had stopped, the steps of one of the cars was immediately in front of him so that he was among the first to board, but those behind pushed him forward until he found himself jammed in the middle of the car by those who had got on at the other end.

The conductor moved ever so slowly through the car, hampered by the tightly packed passengers. He was short and fat, and every now and then he removed his cap to wipe the sweat from his forehead with his sleeve, and this made his progress even slower. The conductor at the other end of the car had stopped to talk to a passenger, so when the train finally pulled into North station at 8:27, the rabbi's ticket had not yet been collected. The conductor was now on the platform, and as the rabbi approached he was going to give him his ticket, but the conductor reached behind him to help an elderly woman out of the car, and the rabbi decided to go with the flow of pedestrian traffic. He was a little bothered at not having paid his fare, but then reflected that perhaps it was recompense for his discomfort in having to stand all the way. At North station, where the trip ended, he took a streetcar to Kenmore Square.

As he emerged from the subway station at Kenmore Square, he was hailed by a young man who looked vaguely familiar. "I don't suppose you remember me, Rabbi," he said. "I was introduced to you at a Friday evening service by Mr. Lerner, who—"

"Oh yes, you're Mr.—er—"

"Jacobs. Mordecai Jacobs."

"Of course. You're going to marry Clara Lerner, and your future father-in-law got me to agree to perform the ceremony. I tried to dissuade him, but—"

"Why would you want to dissuade him?"

"Well, for one thing, his reason for wanting me to do it was that I had married him and Mrs. Lerner, and because their marriage was successful . . ."

"Yeah, that is kind of silly."

"But mostly it was because the wedding was going to take place in Barnard's Crossing, and since I was leaving, there would be another rabbi in charge, and I would thereby be invading his turf, so to speak."

"Oh, I see."

The rabbi smiled. "But now that we are colleagues, I have a more legitimate reason for performing the ceremony, and one that I'm sure Rabbi Selig will understand."

"Well, that's fine then. You going to continue living in Barnard's Crossing? I saw you coming out of the subway, so I guess you must have come in by train or bus today. Is that what you're planning on? Coming in by public transport every day?"

"No, I was planning to drive in most days. But I thought today I'd take the train to avoid the rush-hour traffic. I won't be coming in so early most of the time. My class doesn't meet until eleven. It's just that I thought the first day I ought to come in at the start of classes. I had no idea the train would be so crowded. The conductor didn't even get around to collecting my ticket."

"Yes, it's happened to me on one or two occasions. See, I go to the Lerners' for the weekend, so I have to take the train in Monday morning. It's a drag. You ought to have a pied-à-terre here in the city in case of bad weather during the winter."

"I suppose—"

"Look, Rabbi, I live in Brookline on Beacon Street. It's a big apartment house, nothing fancy, but comfortable. A lot of the folks go down to Florida for the winter, and some of them let their apartments for the winter months. It's right around the corner from Harvard Street, where there's a kosher butcher shop and a synagogue, and it's just across the street from the car stop. And usually the rent isn't very high, I understand, because people don't like to leave their apartments unprotected. Someone living in the apartment is like a caretaker. I was talking to one of the tenants just the other day—"

"It's certainly worth considering."

"Look, if you like, I'll keep my ears open and let you know if I hear of anything."

The rabbi smiled. "I like. I'd appreciate it."

Chapter 11

T H E office that had previously been occupied by half a dozen instructors of Freshman English was large as college offices go. It contained four desks and a couple of tables, all of them old and scarred by years of usage. The rabbi surveyed the room and its furniture and then selected the desk next to a window, which had the most comfortable-looking chair behind it, as his own. It was a large leather chair with a tufted back that tilted when he leaned back, and that could swivel from side to side. The drawers of the desk, he noted with satisfaction, were empty and relatively clean.

The door opened and a young woman, under thirty, came in. She was thin and small with a narrow, freckled face and reddish-blond hair. "Oh, I didn't know there was anyone in here, or I would have knocked," she said.

"Quite all right."

"You must be the rabbi who is going to head up the new Judaica Department."

"I am Rabbi Small, David Small."

"Do I call you Rabbi Small or Professor Small?"

"I'll answer to either one," he said, smiling.

"I'm Sarah McBride, English Department." She pointed to a

desk on the other side of the room. "I used that desk last year. I left some papers in the top drawer. Maybe they're still there."

"I think everything was brought upstairs to the English office," he offered, "but take a look."

She strode to the desk and pulled out the drawer. "Nope. Gone. They're probably upstairs as you say." She leaned back on the desk, facing him. "You going to have a big department?"

The rabbi shrugged. "It will depend on how much interest there is in the field. I'm starting with just me. I'm giving one course this year and I expect it will be small enough to meet in the office here, around a table, seminar style, perhaps. It will be an introductory course—"

"When does it come?"

"It's scheduled for Monday, Wednesday, and Friday at eleven."

"I'm free at eleven. Would you mind if I were to audit your course?" .

"Not at all. Happy to have you. Sarah McBride." He savored the name and smiled. "Not Jewish, I presume."

She smiled. "No, not Jewish. Maybe quite the opposite."

"What do you mean that you're opposite to being Jewish?" asked the rabbi, puzzled.

"Anti-Semitic." She smiled impishly.

"And you want to audit my course . . ."

"To find out why," she replied promptly.

"I don't understand."

"Well, you see, I married one."

"You married a Jew?"

"Uh-huh."

"And now you're separated? Divorced?"

She shook her head. "No, still happily married."

"You were married by a rabbi? A priest? A minister?"

"None of the above. By a justice of the peace. According to

Lew, no rabbi would marry us unless I converted, and he was sure a priest would also demand all kinds of conditions, so . . ."

"It bothered you?"

"Not really. You see, we were in a relationship to begin with."

"You mean you were living together?"

"Uh-huh."

"Without benefit of clergy."

She giggled. "What an old-fashioned phrase."

"Yes, I suppose it is," he said with a sigh. "And after a while you decided to get married?"

"That's right. See, we'd been living together for about a year, and everything was fine. So we decided to get married. But it's not the same. In a relationship, both parties are free. One doesn't have a claim on the other, so each tends to be considerate of the other. But when you're married, you do have a claim, and when it's exercised, the other party is apt to feel aggrieved."

"I don't understand."

"Well, take the matter of living quarters. Lew is a lawyer and he practices in Salem, where he was born and raised. And he lives in your town, in Barnard's Crossing. He bought a house there. I have a studio apartment here in Boston, within walking distance of the school. Well, when we were in a relationship, sometimes I'd go to Barnard's Crossing—weekends mostly, and of course, for the summer. And a couple of times a week he'd come into town to go to dinner and a movie afterwards. Then he'd stay over at my place, of course. And if I was busy, say at exam time, we didn't see each other at all for a couple of days. I mean, it was like falling in love each time we came together. But when we married, he thought we ought to be together all the time. He wants me to give up my apartment and live in Barnard's Crossing."

"It's a very nice place to live," the rabbi remarked.

"Oh sure, but it's no longer fun; it's habit and convenience."

"And you prefer something inconvenient?"

"Well, it's not so convenient for me. I'd have to get up an hour earlier to get to school. We tried it for a while, but it meant that we were together a lot, and when two people are together a lot, they're apt to get on each other's nerves."

"And he began to get on your nerves?"

"Well, the difference in our backgrounds had something to do with it, too. See, when we were in this relationship, I was aware that I was sinning, and when I went to Confession, I mentioned it and did penance for it. But this was different. The other could be considered a momentary urge, a sudden lapse from rectitude. But marrying Lew was making a commitment. It bothered me, and I stopped going to Confession. It was as though in undergoing a secular marriage, I had turned my back on the church."

"And you think he might have felt the same way?"

"Not at all. I would have felt better if he had. But at the most he was a little bothered by what some of his relatives might be thinking. And this—this easygoing attitude of his used to infuriate me. When I had a wicked or evil thought, I felt I had sinned. But not he. He felt he had not sinned unless he had actually done something wrong. He said that's what Jews believe. Is that right?"

The rabbi nodded slowly, judiciously. "Yes, I suppose it is. We realize that the mind has a will of its own. When it is not focused on some particular idea, it wanders off in all directions. That's a fact of the human condition, and we don't beat our heads against reality. We don't try to censor thought any more than we censor books. Was that the only difference?"

"Oh no, it was all sorts of things, even food. I mean, he wasn't observant or anything like that. I mean he didn't go in for all that kosher stuff, like two sets of dishes, but there were things he'd never eaten. When we went out for dinner and I'd order oysters on the half shell as an appetizer, he'd look away. He couldn't watch me eating them. And after we were married and I'd make a

ham steak for dinner, or pork chops, he wouldn't be able to eat.
He'd say he wasn't hungry."

"Early food habits are hard to overcome, I suppose," said the
rabbi.

"Yes, but curiously, he likes lobster. But only in a restaurant.
He won't let me buy them and cook them at home."

"So what happened?"

"So I kept my flat, and during the week I stay there, sometimes
with Lew, and sometimes alone."

"I see, and because sometimes you don't get along with your
husband, you became anti-Semitic?"

She laughed. "Oh, that was just to get a rise out of you. I
thought you might get kind of stuffy if I upset you."

"I see. And if I had, you wouldn't want to audit my course?"

"Oh, I guess I would. I really do want to know what—what
makes you people tick."

"Tick?"

"Yes, you know, what makes you different. I think maybe it's
because you people don't believe things, and we do."

"I'm afraid I don't understand."

"Well, for instance, we're taught to believe in Santa Claus
when we're children. And we're four or five years old before we
get over it. Do you have anything like that?"

"No, I can't say that we have," the rabbi answered, his eyes
twinkling.

"All right. Then we're taught the Adam and Eve story. That because they sinned by eating the apple, all generations of mankind
are born in sin, and if they're not baptized, they'll burn in hell
forever when they die. We're usually in our late teens before we
begin thinking that it's more symbolic than actual, and some of
us go on believing, at least on Sundays. That gives you a head start
on the rest of us: you don't have to believe in anything if it
doesn't make sense. Life is so easy for you. You don't have to

worry about hell all the time. There was a saint or a holy man of some sort in the Middle Ages who never laughed. He said, 'My Lord is crucified and shall I laugh?' Well, we have the feeling that enjoyment, anything that gives us pleasure, is apt to be sinful and may lead to hell. It wouldn't be so bad if yours was one of those strange Eastern religions like Buddhism, say, but ours derives from yours, and your prophets are also ours. But you can enjoy life while we can't. So we're jealous of you. Maybe that's the reason for anti-Semitism."

He smiled. "And you think by taking my course you might learn to disbelieve?"

"You're laughing at me," she said, "but I'm thinking I might get to know Lew better."

Chapter 12

THREE of the four desks and the several tables had been re-moved, and a large, oblong table had been installed instead. A dozen chairs had been set around the table, and the rabbi wheeled his swivel chair over. A blackboard had been installed in a corner: the rabbi wrote his name on it and announced, "I am Rabbi David Small."

He glanced at his class list and said, "On the basis of the names on my list, I presume all of you are Jewish." He smiled. "So we have a minyan."

"There are only nine of us," someone objected.

"And I make the necessary ten," said the rabbi. "Being the tenth man at a minyan has become a function of the American rabbi, I'm afraid."

"But two are girls," the same student objected.

"True, but quite acceptable in liberal Judaism," said the rabbi. "As for those of you who are Orthodox, there is no reason for dis-approval since we are not here to *daven* but to study."

At that point, the door opened and Sarah McBride entered breathless. "I'm sorry," she said, "but I was detained."

"Quite all right," said the rabbi. "This is Ms. McBride, whom some of you may know is in the English Department. She will be auditing the course. And now I shall read off your names, and will you stand or raise your hand when your name is called."

He noted as a matter of minor interest that some of those who had Jewish first names had not Anglicized them. Mosheh did not become Morris or Maurice as it would have a generation ago, or Moses as it would have several generations earlier, and Yitzchak did not become Isaac or Isadore or Irwin. He thought it might portend a greater interest in Judaism, until it occurred to him that Hispanics tended to remain José and did not become Joseph; and that among Italians, Mario tended to be preferred to Mark.

"I arranged for this blackboard to be brought in so that I can make an occasional note for you to copy—mostly names of books or writers. But right now, I'd rather you didn't take notes. For my own purposes, I would like each of you to write a short account of what religious education you have had. List what Religious Schools or Sunday Schools you may have attended, for how long, and the material that you covered."

"What if we didn't go to any?" asked one.

"Then you will say so, of course. But you may have received instruction at home. I'd like you to tell me about that."

"How long?"

"When is it due?"

"Look," said the rabbi, "let's not make a big thing out of this. I'd like it in by the next meeting. And it can be as long as you like: a dozen pages or a single page, or even a paragraph. I don't want an essay on your personal religion, just some indication of your background in Judaism. And by the way, there is no need to raise your hands when you want to say something or ask a question. We're like a committee meeting here, so the common courtesy that you would naturally observe in a small group should be satisfactory. Now let me explain what I have in mind for this course. I intend to outline basic Jewish ideas that are generally agreed to by informed—not necessarily learned—Jews. Informed, rather than scholarly. The distinction is important.

"We are an ancient people with a continuous history covering several thousand years, and since we have never discouraged, much less forbidden, discussion and disagreement, it is inevitable that there should be many, many different views of what Jews should believe. But the fundamental character of the belief cuts across lines of disagreement, and our basic beliefs are fundamentally the same.

"Our religion starts with Chapter Twenty in Exodus, and—"

"Doesn't it start with Genesis, with Adam and Eve?"

The rabbi smiled. "No, those are myths and fables attempting to explain our origins on earth. All people wonder about two things: how they got here, that is, how mankind got here on earth, and how evil came about. For example, the ancient Greeks attributed the origin of man to Prometheus and explained the presence of evil by the legend of Pandora's box. Characteristically, perhaps, we explain it by disobedience to God's commandment. The stories of Abraham, Isaac, and Jacob, and later Joseph, however, probably have some historical validity. And I say this because all have faults. If they were purely legendary, if they were merely thought up, I don't think we would have included their faults.

"In any case, we believe that we derive from them, the so-called Fathers, just as we believe that we were chosen by God to be a light unto the nations."

"Do you believe that?"

The rabbi shrugged. "It's a common enough belief among nations that they have a special mission with respect to the rest of the world. The Greeks thought they alone were civilized and all other people were barbarians or savages. The Romans thought it was their duty to spread the benefits of Roman law and order to the rest of the world. The Spaniards thought their function was to spread Catholicism, and the English felt that they were conferring the benefits of Victorian England on India and Africa. Our own country feels a mission to spread democracy, just as, until very recently, the Russians thought it was their function to spread communism. And then there is Islam, which once again feels it has a special mission. The big difference is that we were enjoined to do it by force of example rather than by the sword. You may ridicule the idea that an Almighty God would select one group of people from all the rest, but the fact is that that group believed it, and more or less acted accordingly."

A student ventured, "Is that the official view?"

"How do you mean 'official'?" asked the rabbi.

"Well, you know, the accepted version of the Jewish church or synagogue, or whatever you call it?"

"If you're thinking of an official creed," said the rabbi, "we don't have one. Every synagogue is autonomous. And every Jew tends to interpret the Law as he sees fit, as it applies to himself. We have laws governing our dealings with others, but we are free to use our minds without restraint or censorship. Someone else, another rabbi, or any other Jew, might find my interpretation entirely unacceptable, but he would not repudiate my right to my opinion."

"And women, do they have the right to interpret the Law?" asked one of the female students.

"That's not really a question, is it, Ms. Goldman? I mean, it wasn't asked to elicit a definite answer. It was asked in order to point out discrimination against women in Judaism. Wasn't it? This discrimination is apt to refer to such things as the separation of the sexes in the synagogue—"

"The women have to sit in a balcony, behind a curtain yet," said Ms. Goldman with indignation.

"Only in Orthodox synagogues," the rabbi pointed out, "and

old-fashioned ones at that. The idea is that the sight of the women might distract the men from their prayers. You could argue that it is complimentary to women. It was not so long ago that practically all colleges were either for men or for women; only state colleges were coeducational."

"My grandfather said the public schools were segregated by sex, too," a student volunteered. "Girls sat on one side of the room and boys on the other."

"Yeah, there was a picture in the textbook we used in Education 101 last year," said another.

The rabbi nodded. "Does that explain it for you, Ms. Goldman? If you look into the matter in depth, I think you'll find that women have what many would regard as a preferred position in Judaism. The center of our religion is not the synagogue, but the home, and there the woman is obviously in command. And then there is the matter of the Ketubah. *What* is a Ketubah, anyone?"

"It's the marriage contract, isn't it?" said a student.

"That's right, Mr.—er—"

"Ritter. Asher Ritter."

"You're quite right, Mr. Ritter. But it's a one-way contract. It gives the duties of the groom and the promises he makes to the bride, but there is no corresponding list of obligations and promises of the bride to the groom."

"But he can divorce her, if he wants to," said the other female student.

"Not unless she is willing to accept the bill of divorcement, Ms. Sachs," said the rabbi. "Not since the ruling of Rabbi Gershom in the eleventh century. Originally we were a polygamous society, as were all other societies at the time. But we have made changes in our rules, or reinterpreted them, to conform to more modern habits of thought. And those changes give us an insight to the general attitude of our people.

"The emphasis in this course will be not on reading or research, but on thought. Much of what we know, or think we know, is based on something we've heard or read. I think that's the trouble with modern scholarship and collegiate study all the way up to the doctorate. I'm going to ask you to think about the material we will be dealing with rather than memorizing what someone has said about it. So I'd rather you didn't take notes in this class. Listen and think about what I say or what any one of your classmates says. And don't be afraid of disagreeing with me. I'll appreciate the compliment of your thinking about it and arriving at another conclusion."

He paused and looked at them to see if they had understood. "And to give you a little practice, your assignment for next time—"

"You've already given us an assignment for next time."

"That wasn't really an assignment; merely a chance to introduce yourselves to me. But all right, this will be for Monday, almost a week from today. It will give you a little practice in what we've been talking about. According to Isaiah, we were to be a light unto the nations. Well, have we been? I want you to think about it and be prepared to report on it, in detail, at our Monday meeting."

As they trooped out of the room, the students discussed the class and the rabbi. "What do you think? Think he's going to make us work?"

"Well, the guy that signed my program, my adviser, said he didn't think he'd be likely to give a snap course."

"Look, it's an elementary course, so if you've been to Hebrew School—you have, haven't you?—what can he teach you, you don't already know?"

"So why take the course?"

"Well, maybe he's got like a new slant on it. Besides, it'll please my old man."

"You got a point there. Maybe when I talk to my mom, I'll tell her and she'll be able to brag about it to her bridge group."

Chapter 13

SARAH McBride lingered on to explain, to apologize. "I'm sorry I was late, Rabbi, but the English office is a crazy place on the first day of classes. I suppose the other offices are, too. But Professor Kent said he simply had to have a book, a catalog of some kind, and I was free at the moment, so I had to go."

"Busy, was he?"

"No, just bossy. Usually he has Professor Miller running his errands, but Miller is an adviser, *L* to *P*, I think. You know, they're supposed to check student programs to see if they're eligible for the courses they've selected. So he couldn't go."

"Professor Kent is head of your department?"

"No, that's Bob Sugrue. Professor Kent is—well, he's important. I don't know why. You see, I'm kind of new here, but I know he's important by the way he acts and how others act towards him."

"And Professor Miller is his assistant?"

"I don't think it's anything official, but they're together a lot." She glanced at her watch. "Oh, I'd better get going if I'm going to get any lunch. I've a one-o'clock. How about you? You going to the cafeteria?"

"I'm afraid not. I can't eat—"

"Oh, you mean you've got to eat kosher. Well, they have salads and soups. Those are all right, aren't they?"

"Probably, but for today at least I'll just have the sandwich my wife prepared."

"Well, then I'll be going." At the door she stopped. "Oh, Professor Fine heard I was auditing your course and asked me to say hello for him and that he'd drop by first chance he gets. He's an adviser, too. You know him, don't you?"

"He married a girl from Barnard's Crossing and I officiated at his wedding."

It was after he had finished his sandwich that Professor Roger Fine poked his red head through the door and called out, "Greetings, Rabbi. Colleagues again! I see you've finished your lunch," as the rabbi crumpled the plastic wrapper that had contained his sandwich. "How about coming down to the faculty cafeteria for a cup of coffee?"

The rabbi stood up. "Sounds good." And then as they headed for the door, "You don't need your cane anymore?"

"Only if I have to walk some distance. I carry it coming here and going home, but I don't need it while I'm in the building. Lord knows I can use a cup of coffee. We've got an electric percolator up in the English office, but the cups are never properly washed, just rinsed, and in any case I want to get away from my desk. I'm an adviser—to all students whose names begin with *A* through *E.* Upperclassmen know better, of course, but freshmen think I am there to actually give them advice. 'I want to study the environment, so should I take French or Spanish?' Nowadays, they're all concerned about the environment, and whales and dolphins, and the spotted owl."

"I suppose every generation has to have its special cause. In my day it was civil rights and blacks," the rabbi remarked.

The faculty cafeteria, when they arrived, was almost empty.

"Not too many here," observed the rabbi. "Is it the food?"

"Oh, no. It's the hour. At noon you'd have trouble finding a table. But by one o'clock, the place is as it is now, practically empty. It fills up again around three, and they have a fair number till seven, the late-afternoon and evening classes."

"Late-afternoon classes, a special group?"

"Oh, yes. Extension courses. Schoolteachers mostly. See, they get extra credit and higher pay when they take courses. And because we're situated where we can be easily reached, especially by streetcar, we do very well. Of course, we also get a lot of people who are not schoolteachers, you know, retired people."

They went to the counter, received their cups of coffee, and then sat down at a small table in the center of the room. Another pair entered the room, and Fine murmured, "Ah, the Odd Couple."

The rabbi looked up. "The Odd Couple?"

"Yeah, Miller and Kent. That's what we call them. They're always together."

Professor Kent acknowledged their presence with a nod, but his younger companion, Professor Miller, waved and called out, "Hi, Roger." Instead of joining them, however, Professor Kent marched determinedly to a table in the far corner of the room while Miller went to the counter to get coffee for both of them.

"Odd because of the difference in their ages?"

"Well, that, too. But Kent is always bragging about the important people he knows because he was married to the last of the Clarks, and Miller is a nobody from North Dakota or Nebraska. And since neither of them is a scholar, it can't be because they are engaged in some research together. I can understand Miller, sort of. Because Kent lives in that big house on the corner and was married to Matilda Clark, he thinks he is aristocracy. And he thinks it was Kent that got him tenure, so he's grateful."

."And could he have got tenure through Kent's influence?"

Fine shrugged. "I don't know. According to Bob Sugrue, our

department head who is a friend of one of the members of the Board of Trustees, the college handles Kent with kid gloves because of that house he lives in. It was willed to the college by his wife, but Kent can throw a monkey wrench into the works; dower rights, or some such thing. So they let him stay on although he's beyond the retirement age. And when a female member of the department complained of sexual harassment, because he's a lecherous old bugger, it was the woman who left. We had three and now we've only got one, Sarah McBride. And I'm waiting for the day when her husband, Lew, comes to see him and tells him he'll break his arm if he doesn't stop pawing his wife."

Chapter 14

WHEN the International Correspondence School, head-quartered in St. Louis, decided to open a branch office in London, with the vague notion of perhaps establishing it as their head office since London would carry more prestige than St. Louis, Michael Canty, who had been with the company since graduating from high school five years before, managed to get himself included in the small crew that was being sent over. He had started as an office boy and was now one of the correspondence clerks at no great increase in salary. But whereas he had formerly run errands, filed, dusted, and gone out for coffee, he now corrected papers and wrote letters. No special knowledge was required for either function: the answers the students sent in were matched against the approved answers; and the letters consisted of selecting and arranging prewritten paragraphs in a letter of encouragement or approval.

He rented a room in a boardinghouse not far from the company office. There was a double hot plate in the room, and even a couple of pots and a few dishes, but except for an occasional pot of tea, he ate in one of the many pubs or cheap restaurants nearby. In the evening he usually sought out free entertainment, lectures, a church service, or the Visitors' Gallery in the House of

Commons when Parliament was in session. He couldn't afford the theater or a nightclub on his salary. Sometimes he was able to make the acquaintance of a girl, and once in a while persuaded one to spend the night with him.

He received an occasional increase in salary, but they were very small increases because the enterprise did not prosper. When at the end of seven years, it was decided to close the London branch, Mike Canty was still living in the same boardinghouse.

But he had himself undergone some change. He had gradually lost his flat midwestern accent, at first unconsciously, and then consciously as he realized that in England it had social significance. He was particularly bothered about his name, Michael, or more commonly, Mike Canty. He felt that it had a low-class ring to it. He experimented with Canté and Cantay. Finally he changed it to Malcolm Kent.

He could have gone back to St. Louis, and he was quite certain that if he did, he would be offered a job in the head office. But he had been with the company for over ten years, and what had it got him? On the other hand, what hope had he, an American, of getting a job with an English company? No, he would return to the States, but not to St. Louis; he would go to New York, or Boston, or Philadelphia, somewhere on the coast. He finally decided on Boston because there was a direct flight there from Heathrow, and because he had heard that it was a little like an English city.

He found a room on Beacon Hill, and spent a few days in walking around the city. It was late August and the weather was balmy. Armed with a map of the city, he visited the Public Gardens and the Esplanade, and the Common where people made speeches from portable lecterns to passersby on Marxism, militant Christianity, and flat earth geography, quite like London's Hyde Park.

But soon he decided he had to find a job. He studied the want ads in the newspapers and visited each of the employment agencies listed in the yellow pages of the telephone directory. He stood in lines; he filled out forms.

He had no trade, seemingly no skills at all. For clerical jobs, women were preferred. As for jobs that called for physical strength or stamina, he did not have the build for them. He was a little below average in height—five inches above five feet—and he was thin and scrawny. His thin face with deep-set eyes, short, straight nose, and pointed chin was attractive, even good-looking, but not marketable.

There were a number of ads for salesmen, but most paid on a commission basis, and usually involved the need for a car.

In the Sunday paper he noticed a small, discreet ad for the "Williams Teachers' Agency, Ada Williams, Manager." It offered no indication that jobs were available, and he suspected that payment of a fee was necessary for registration. But finding himself on School Street one day where the agency was located, he decided to inquire. After all, he had been in the teaching business, hadn't he?

The agency occupied a suite of two rooms: the outer room had a desk and several wooden armchairs, and was presumably occupied by a secretary, possibly out to lunch since it was noon. The door to the inner office was open, and a tall, handsome woman sitting behind a mahogany desk invited him to come in and sit down.

He explained that he had worked for a correspondence school in London but had not ever engaged in classroom instruction. He implied without saying so explicitly that he had made up lessons and examinations, although his work had in fact been purely clerical.

"This was in the field of English?"

"Yes, language and literature."

"Did you ever take courses in Education?"

"In Education?"

She smiled. "I see you haven't. I'm afraid you can't teach in a public school, not in this state, unless you have had a course in Education." He looked so disappointed that she added, "You could take an extension course at one of the colleges, or go to Summer School."

"But then I wouldn't be eligible until next year," he protested.

"Of course, colleges don't require Education courses, and neither do private schools. Colleges usually require a graduate degree, however," she said.

"And private schools?"

"I'm afraid they don't pay very much."

"I don't mind. It would give me a start, and I could use the experience in applying for another job. It's just that I'd like to get started."

She nodded to show she was sympathetic; he was so eager, so anxious. "It's late in the season and I don't have a job in my books right now. Of course, something might come in at the last minute: a teacher gets sick or resigns to take another job." She hesitated for a moment, and then with a decided shake of her head in rejection of a thought that had occurred to her, she said, "But the chances of a job coming in that you could fill are so remote that I don't think it would be even worth your while to register. The fee is ten dollars, but I don't suppose . . ."

"Not if it's so unlikely." He rose. "Well, thank you for taking the time."

"It's what I'm here for."

He was at the door when she called out. "Oh, Mr. Kent, I just remembered something."

He turned expectantly.

"I was at a conference a couple of weeks ago and met the dean of Windermere College, a Millicent Hanbury. She mentioned that enrollment seemed to be going up sharply and they might have to get another instructor for Freshman English. Windermere is not a client of mine, and she didn't ask me to find one for her. I'm not sure that she knew I ran a teachers' agency. But there's a chance. It used to be a ladies' finishing school, a sort of junior college. It had a very small regular faculty. Most of the courses were given by local high school teachers who'd come to teach a class or two and then go back to their regular schools. Then it became a four-year women's college, and I guess their standards went up some. Then it became coeducational and their enrollment began to climb. It's in the city on Clark Road near Kenmore Square."

"Should I call for an appointment first?"

"If you call, her secretary is apt to put you off. Why don't you just go over there."

"All right, I will."

"Oh, and if you should get the job, Mr. Kent, our fee is ten percent of the first year's salary."

"I'll be more than happy to pay it."

"And of course, the ten-dollar registration fee."

❖   ❖   ❖

The possibility, much less the likelihood, of his getting a job, he reasoned, was remote, else Ada Williams would have required him to register and pay the ten-dollar fee. But the day was warm and pleasant, so he thought he might as well walk to Kenmore Square; he had nothing else to do.

As he walked along, he thought about the interview. If there was a job, and if he did have a chance, he would no doubt be asked about his college and what degree he held. So much was certain if for no other reason than that it had to appear beside his name in the catalog. So he decided he would lie.

It was fairly safe, he felt. If he was asked for his diploma or certificate of graduation, he would say it was in his trunk that was being shipped from England. Would they phone or cable the university? Most unlikely, but they might write. It would be a week before the letter would arrive in England, and weeks, perhaps months, before the university would reply. Even then, if confronted with the letter from the university, he would explain that he had changed his name from Michael Canty to Malcolm Kent and that the degree had been granted to the former. More correspondence, and by the time it was over, it would be so far into the semester that they wouldn't dare drop him.

Clark Street was a short, tree-lined street with a row of three-story brownstone-front houses on either side. All were of much the same size except for one house on the corner that seemed almost twice as large as any of the other houses. But it was the building marked "Administration" several doors down that commanded his interest and to which he headed.

❖ ❖ ❖

He could see right away that Millicent Hanbury found his British accent attractive. "Miss Eastland is head of the English Department," she said, "and normally she'd be the one you'd see, but she's away and won't be back until the day before school starts, so she asked me to pick someone. It's only for Freshman English, and of course, there's no tenure."

"I'll take it if I can get it," he said.

"And your degree is from . . . ?"

"London Polytech."

"Oh. A.B. or B.S.?"

"A.B., but my master's is from University of Liverpool," he added to complicate things.

❖ ❖ ❖

Freshman English instructors—there were no professors—had an office apart from the rest of the English faculty since the course involved conferences with students on their themes, the writing of which was the principal function of the course. Naturally, there was considerable fraternizing among the Freshman English instructors since they shared an office. There was a good deal of talk among them about their respective schools, about the professors under whom they had studied, about the various requirements for graduate study.

Kent, however, tended to keep apart from his colleagues. When asked a direct question, he would answer with a monosyllable. And he did not hang around the office unless he was waiting for a student. Instead, he would go to the school library and read, or wander through the stacks, picking a book off the shelves that looked interesting. His colleagues attributed his unfriendliness to the fact that he was a bit older—they had got their degrees only the year before—or perhaps because he was British. Some thought he was a natural grouch, and others that he spent so much time in the library because he was engaged in research. His real reason, however, for not engaging in their chitchat was that he was afraid he might say something that would indicate that he had never gone to college. It was hard for him since he was by nature sociable and talkative. So he did as he had done in London: he went to lectures and concerts and evening services at local churches.

After a few years he was promoted from instructor to assistant professor. Now, as Professor Kent, he taught several sections of the Survey of English Literature course as well as a section of the Freshman English course.

Over the years, the status of the school had improved, steadily although almost imperceptibly. The doctorate became required of most appointees to the faculty, and after a while, in several departments, publication in learned journals as proof of scholarship was also required. The status of the school, which formerly had been on a par with one of the local junior colleges, was now thought to be equal to the state four-year college.

Then the president, Allen Treadwell Chisholm, retired, and Donald Macomber, a historian of some repute, was installed in his place. Although still regarded as a fallback school for the prestigious Ivy League colleges of the area, it was also attracting students for whom it was the first choice, in part because tuition fees were considerably lower than those of the Ivy League colleges, and in part because admission standards were more liberal.

But as the status of the college increased, Kent's status with his colleagues diminished correspondingly. When he had first joined the faculty, academically he had been thought to be more or less on a par with the other members of the faculty, who had been high school teachers or instructors in local colleges. There had been no Ph.D.s in the English Department; the president had been a high school principal; and Dean Millicent Hanbury had been head of the Physical Education Department.

But now, almost all professors had Ph.D.s, and most of them had published in learned journals. There were even some who were held in esteem by their colleagues in other colleges. And Professor Kent? He stayed on because there was no reason to dismiss him.

And then he met Matilda Clark. She was the great-granddaughter of Ezra Clark, who had built the row of brownstone fronts on the street that was named for him and who was not only one of the founders of Windermere, but the donor of one of the houses on Clark Street, the first building of the college. She was a spinster of fifty, five or six years older than he, and lived in the big corner house, where she had been born.

On a cold, blustery winter's day, as he was walking along Clark Street, leaning forward against the buffeting of the wind, he had caught sight of her clinging to the iron railing on the steps of her house. He hurried toward her and asked if he could help her. She nodded gratefully and he helped her up the steps. She handed him her key and he opened the door. Then, inside, in gratitude she offered him tea.

"I get sort of short-winded sometimes," she explained as she led him to a small, nondescript room off the entrance hall.

"Everyone does sometimes," he assured her.

"Oh, is that so? This was my study when I was going to school," she said, "and I like to eat in here because it's near the kitchen. If you'll wait here, I'll bring the tea things. I won't be long."

He looked about him when she left. There were a couple of chairs and a table, the one she used to study at, presumably. There was a small bookcase against the wall, and he walked over to examine the books it contained. They were the books she had used in grammar school and perhaps high school. He picked up a copy of *Macbeth*, and was leafing through it, trying to read the penciled notes in the margins, when she returned carrying a tray with two cups, each containing a tea bag, and a plate of cookies.

"You don't use a teapot?" he asked.

"Too much work," she answered.

"You don't have any help?"

"No. I like to do for myself. If I didn't keep house, and cook, what would I do all day?" She noticed the book in his hand and said, "That's Shakespeare. Would you like to borrow it?"

It occurred to him that if he borrowed a book from her, it would be an excuse to come again to return it, so he said, "Yes. I'm not familiar with this edition."

"So take it."

"I'll bring it back tomorrow."

"All right."

"Look, I have a class that ends at four o'clock. Why don't I come tomorrow and I'll make tea for you, English tea, in a teapot with milk."

"Oh, that would be nice."

As they talked over their tea, he could see that she was not very bright, and he began to realize the enormous possibilities her simplicity offered.

The very next day, shortly after four, he presented himself at the Clark house with the book he had borrowed under his arm, and in a bag, a tin of English breakfast tea and a ceramic teapot. When she opened the door in response to his ring, he said, "I've come to return your book and to make you a cup of real English tea. You have milk, haven't you?"

"Yes, I have milk. Come in."

She stayed by his side in the kitchen as he explained, "The water must be bubbling furiously. That's important. And then it must steep for seven minutes. Then you just add a dash of milk to the cup. That absorbs the tannin, you understand. Now, if you'll go into the study, I'll serve you your tea."

She sipped cautiously at the cup he set before her. "Oh, that's good," she exclaimed.

"It's the way tea should be made," he said.

As they drank their tea, she prattled about friends she had grown up with and what they were doing now, about charitable organizations she supported because they had always been supported by her father and grandfather. And he listened, every now and then throwing in a sentence or two to encourage her to go on. He stayed until almost six and then left for a bite of supper, after which he went to a singles bar and picked up a woman whom he induced to come home with him.

He came almost every day and occasionally stayed for supper. She expected to see him every day, and on one occasion when he explained that he would not be able to come for tea since there was an important departmental meeting that he had to attend, she said, "Then come for lunch. I'll expect you."

It was while he was having lunch that he heard the postman push the mail through the slot. He went to the front door and picked it off the floor, then brought it back to the table. It consisted mostly of advertisements, of course, but there was one envelope that looked important and he remarked on it.

She opened it and said, "It's an invitation. I get them quite often."

"And don't you go?"

"Sometimes. Oh, this one is from the Sloans. He was a partner of my father in some deal. This is for the evening of the twenty-fourth."

"Are you going?"

"He's just been appointed chairman of the Arts Commission. I don't like to go without an escort, especially in the evening."

"I could take you."

"It's formal."

"Well, I have a dinner jacket, you know, a tuxedo."

"All right, if you don't mind. We were awfully close to the Sloans at one time. I'll be able to see a lot of people I used to know, but it might be awfully dull for you; there'll be a lot of speeches."

"I don't mind, if you think you'll enjoy it."

Although the time of his visits to the Clark house was after most of the faculty had gone home, nevertheless, he had been observed, and some who taught extension classes had seen him leaving. In a curious way, he sensed that it had given him a new importance. When he talked about some of the people he had met—for after the Sloan party, he had squired Matilda Clark to other affairs—his colleagues were inclined to listen. For example, when the press reported on the changes Harvey Challenger was planning for the public library system and his colleagues in the English Department were discussing them, he was able to say, "The man is an idiot."

"You know him?"

"I met him at a party."

But it was more than that. Seemingly, it was not the important people he met through Matilda Clark, but his friendship with the lady herself, that was giving him importance. It occurred to him that perhaps it was assumed that she had influence with the Board of Trustees. He decided to test it.

At his next meeting with her, he remarked that he had been offered a job in the Midwest, and that he was thinking of taking it.

"Oh, you mustn't do that. You mustn't leave Windermere."

"I'm not doing very well here. I'm only an assistant professor, and I don't even have tenure after all the years I've been here."

"Why, that's terrible. I'll tell you what: I'll speak to Charlie Dobson."

"Charlie Dobson? Who's he?"

"He has that big Cadillac agency on Commonwealth Avenue, and he's on the Board of Trustees." She reflected for a moment and then said, "The next quarterly meeting of the Board is in a couple of weeks, so I'll go to see him tomorrow. He'll need a little time to contact the others, you know."

Among the many announcements that were made following the meeting of the Board was one that Assistant Professor Malcolm Kent had been promoted to associate professor and granted tenure.

With his promotion and its accompanying tenure, he no longer worried that his lack of academic background might be discovered. Even if by some fluke it were found that he had no degree, would the college dare to admit it after he had taught there for so many years and was now an associate professor? It would reflect on the academic standing of all the students who had passed under his hand.

Since he now taught a couple of sections in the survey course, he was able to move into the regular English office, although he retained a desk in the Freshman English office. His colleagues there were older, nearer his own age, and he spent considerable time there, participating in the conversation.

His colleagues there considered him something of a bore since he was always talking about the important people he knew, but they were careful not to show their distaste because he was thought to have influence with the trustees, and a disparaging word from him might affect their chances of promotion. It was thought that this influence was because of his friendship with Matilda Clark, whom none of them knew, but all were aware that she had clout.

Since getting his promotion, he had no doubt of it himself, and was careful to keep the friendship alive. Hardly a day went by that he did not contrive to see her, if only for a few minutes to drop off a magazine or a newspaper clipping that he thought might interest her. And she seemed equally anxious to see him. He was someone she could prattle to, or even sit silently with as she watched a video.

❖   ❖   ❖

Once as they were having tea and talking about a reception they had attended the day before, he asked, "Do these friends of yours ever ask you about me?"

"Of course they do."

"And what do you tell them?"

She giggled. "I tell them you're my fiancé."

"And what do they say to that?"

"Oh, they think it's wonderful and want to know when we're going to get married."

"Well, how about it?"

"How about getting married, you mean? It might be kind of nice; you'd be here all the time. But I don't think I could stand the—you know, the nasty stuff."

"The nasty stuff?"

"You know, in bed."

If she had had the slightest physical appeal for him, he might have tried to persuade her that what happened in bed was not nasty. Instead, he nodded gravely and said, "I feel the same way you do. It's really for young people who want to have children."

At the end of the school year, when he was forty-eight and she was fifty-four, they were married by a justice of the Massachusetts Supreme Court. And seemingly as a wedding gift from the college, he was promoted to the rank of full professor. Because it was more or less expected, they went on a honeymoon to Penobscot Bay in Maine. When they came up to their room after dinner, he was not surprised to find that she had arranged with the hotel manager to replace their king-sized bed with twin beds. When they came back to Boston and he moved into the Clark house, he was not displeased when he saw that they were to occupy separate bedrooms.

"You like to read at night," she explained, "and the light keeps me awake."

"All right. It's probably better this way."

The marriage was never consummated. It was a businesslike partnership rather than a marriage. He would have breakfast and lunch at the faculty dining room, but come home in the late afternoon for tea with her. Then he would read or prepare his lectures in the privacy of his bedroom while she would go about the business of making dinner. When he suggested that perhaps they ought to have a housekeeper, she said, "Then what will I do? I like keeping house. It keeps me busy. It gives me something to do."

Occasionally they ate out and went to a movie or the theater afterward.

He had assumed early in their acquaintance that she had an income commensurate with the grand house she lived in. But as their friendship grew, she had confided in him more and more, and he discovered that all that remained of the Clark fortune was a moderate income.

"Daddy willed his estate to the college, all except this house. And they send me a check every month. It's what they call an annuity. I guess he thought if he left me, you know, his portfolio of stocks and bonds, I wouldn't be able to manage it. I wouldn't know when to sell and what to hold on to if it went down for a while. He had somebody doing it for him, a company, but he didn't trust them to do it for me the same way. I mean, he was always checking with them, and they'd talk it over with him. But, of course, I couldn't do that."

Although disappointing, the monthly check was quite sizable. To be sure, a large part of it she used to contribute to the charities her father, and her grandfather, too, had always supported; it was a sort of family obligation. Still, there was enough left, in combination with his own salary and the fact that he no longer had rent to pay, to keep him very comfortably off. In fact, it made him feel positively affluent. For one thing, since he was something of a dandy, it enabled him to expand his wardrobe considerably.

Then the barbershop he patronized engaged a manicurist. She was small and cuddly with blond hair cut short in a Dutch clip, but combed back from her forehead. He judged that she was not yet thirty. She was flirtatious with her clients, especially those who were good tippers. He had her do his nails whenever he came in for a haircut, and he tipped lavishly.

Like most barbershops, this one was closed on Mondays since they worked a full day on Saturday, and of particular interest to Kent was that she was free all day Monday. In a short while he became a friend rather than a client or customer, and instead of tipping her, he would bring her little gifts, a pair of earrings, a pin, and slide them unobtrusively across the table to her. And they now called each other by their given names, Malcolm and Lorraine.

Once he invited her to lunch on a Monday, and when she

agreed, he said he would pick her up at her flat. He arrived a little before nine while she was still in her nightgown and a hastily donned bathrobe.

"What time is it? I haven't had my breakfast yet. I thought you said we were going to lunch," she said.

"Oh, did I say lunch? I meant brunch. And I brought it with me so you shouldn't have to prepare it," he said gaily, and proceeded to empty the paper bag he'd brought with him: thin-sliced pumpernickel, rolls, smoked salmon, cheeses, and a bottle of wine. He called the English Department and asked them to put up a notice that he would not meet his ten-o'clock class, and then later in the day he called again to say that he would not meet his afternoon class either. They didn't go out to lunch, but made do with what he had brought and what she had in the refrigerator, and she never got around to getting dressed.

When he got home a little after four, he looked tired, and his wife asked if he'd had a hard day. He shook his head dolefully and said, "I spent the whole day at Widener Library. There was something I simply had to work out."

Although he thought of Monday as Lorraine's Day, and made a point of seeing her every Monday, it was not like the first time. He was, after all, in his mid-fifties and she was not yet thirty; her demands were beyond his capacity. So now, when he arranged with her for lunch, he came around noon. Instead of calling the English Department to cancel his afternoon class, he used it as a reason for leaving. They would sit around in her apartment, or in a restaurant if they had gone out to eat, and she would talk about her customers or of things that had happened in the shop, of the barbers, their jealousies, of what they said when a customer gave a tip they considered too small.

He found it interesting, and he developed a genuine affection for her that had nothing to do with going to bed with her. She had become like a young sister or a daughter. He was not the least bit upset or annoyed or even disappointed when one Monday morning she called the English office and asked him not to come. He assumed she had something she had to do, shopping perhaps. He saw her at the barbershop the following Friday, and as she did his nails, she said, "Oh, I can't see you this next Monday, Malcolm. Do you mind?"

"No. It so happens I've got a lot of work to do."

The Monday after that, she asked him to meet her at the restaurant they frequented rather than pick her up at her flat. "I've got to be in that neighborhood in the morning. The dressmaker in the block is making some alterations on a dress I bought."

All through their lunch, she prattled as she usually did. When their coffee was served, he asked, "You saw somebody else last Monday?"

For a moment, she was silent as she considered. Then she nodded.

"And the Monday before that?"

"Uh-huh. Tony."

"Tony? Who's Tony?"

"Tony Donofrio, the middle chair. He wants to marry me."

"And do you want to marry him?"

"I'm going to have a baby."

"Is it mine or his?"

"I don't know," she wailed.

He drummed the table as he asked, "Does he, this Tony, know about us?" Curiously, he was not the least bit jealous. He suspected she might have been carrying on with Tony for some time. Maybe even with others. After all, she was not restricted to Mondays.

"He thinks we're related, that you're my mother's cousin."

He nodded. "Very good." And it occurred to him that it was good. Otherwise, it could become embarrassing. She might start calling him at home; or even call on him. She might even go to see Matilda to get her to divorce him.

"You won't be able to go on working soon. Can he support you?"

"Well, Tony thinks we should go into business together. He'll be the hairdresser. He can do ladies' hair. That's what he trained for originally. And I'll do the manicures. He's got a friend who has a hairdresser place in Lynn—really his father's friend—and he's pretty old and wants to retire to Florida. It's right near the train station and he'll sell it for just about the cost of the fixtures. Two chairs, he's got, and Tony says they're in good condition, practically new."

"But near the train station, is that a good location for a hairdresser?"

"Oh, but that's the beauty part of it, according to Tony. See, there was a shoe factory right in the next block, and they're converting it to condominiums, which will not be too expensive, and should fill up right away. So there'll be a couple of hundred customers right around the block within walking distance, and no trouble finding a place to park. Tony is dickering with the old geezer. He wants a little more than we've got and he won't take a note for the difference. Wants it all cash. But as soon as we strike a deal, we'll get married."

"How far apart are you?"

"About a thousand dollars. If we can work something out with the bank . . ."

"You'd move to Lynn?"

"Yeah, that's where Tony lives. His father works for the city in the Highway Department. He's got lots of folks there. He thinks maybe he could borrow the money from him, or his friends."

"I'll lend you the money."

"You will? Gee, Malcolm. That's wonderful. I'll tell Tony to-morrow. He'll be thrilled."

"And I won't charge you any interest." He thought for a moment and then said, "You'll sign a note, you and this Tony—what's his name?"

"Donofrio."

"You and Tony Donofrio. For six months. If you can't pay it by then, I'll extend it. I just want to make sure everything goes the way you're planning."

"Swell! You'll come to the wedding, won't you?"

"I'll try."

"And—er—Mrs. Kent?"

He shook his head slowly. "I don't think so. She's not well. Cancer."

"Oh, I am sorry."

She was a year in dying, and the college took care of her all through her illness. When she found that she could no longer do housework, they supplied a housekeeper, a Mrs. Bell, who came every day to tidy up and to cook their meals. At critical times, they engaged nurses to take care of her. When she died at the age of sixty, the flags on the college buildings were lowered to half-mast.

With her death, the annuity stopped, but it was no great loss to Kent. Most of the money she had contributed to the causes that her father and grandfather had supported, and the rest she had spent largely on herself. Financially, he was quite comfortable since he was now receiving the salary of a full professor, and with no rent to pay. The college continued to have Mrs. Bell come in for an hour or so a day to keep the house clean and to cook an occasional meal for him.

With his wife gone, Kent felt strangely alone. He had had no great love for her, but he had got used to her, and now he missed her in the same way, perhaps, as he might miss a favorite easy chair or even a favorite pair of slippers. He could always count on her being at home, so that he never felt alone.

He considered her not too intelligent, and not well read; her reading was confined to what he regarded as trashy magazines with a great many pictures. But she knew quite a bit about some of the important families of Boston and she could gossip about them. Sometimes they would go out for dinner to a nearby restaurant, or to a movie, but most of the time they stayed home, silent for the most part, to be sure, but occasionally over a cup of tea or coffee, they would talk about people she used to know. She would spot a name in the newspaper and then tell him about the time she had gone to the person's country home with her father when she was a little girl.

And he had no friends in the college. His colleagues found him a bore. His scholarship was negligible, so he hesitated to talk about books and literature. It seemed his talk was all boasting—of important people he had had some contact with, of some important affair he had attended, of what he had said to a congressman, to the chairman of a commission. And they avoided him because they feared him: he had some sort of influence, some sort of "drag" with the trustees of the college; they weren't sure why except that it was through his wife, and it might be used to their detriment.

He thought of the Donofrios in Lynn as his family, and was invited to dinner to celebrate the birth of their daughter Josephine—"If it had been a boy, we would have called him Malcolm," Lorraine had told him. And afterward to each of her birthdays. When she was old enough to talk, the child was taught to call him "Uncle Malcolm," but he sensed that Tony had no strong liking for him, might even be suspicious of him.

Occasionally Tony came to Boston to borrow money from him, for an unforeseen plumbing bill, for an oil bill, to meet an insurance payment. It was never for a large sum, a few hundred dollars at most. Since he did not schedule clients after four o'clock in the afternoon, he would usually leave shortly after, walk the short distance to the railroad station, and make the train that left at twenty past. In Boston he might stop off somewhere for a cup of coffee just to waste time, and arrive at the English office of the college at a quarter of five. There he would wait until Kent was finished with his four-o'clock class. Sometimes Kent finished his class early, in which case Tony would go to his house on the corner. He never called up in advance to say he was coming because he was afraid that Kent would pretend to be busy and would be unable to see him.

Although Tony was the same age as Lorraine, he looked older, at least, more mature. He was tall and muscular with dark eyes set in a square face. His jet black hair was combed so that a wave hung over his forehead. He had a square jaw and the heavy nose of a boxer. The tunic he wore in the shop had short sleeves that showed strong, hairy forearms much admired by his clients.

The first time he had come, Roger Fine was the only one in the English office, and he asked politely, "Is there something I can do for you?"

"I want to see Professor Kent."

"He should be along any minute now. You a friend of his?"

"My wife's uncle."

"Oh. Well, his class ends at five. That's his desk over there. Why don't you sit there until he comes."

Kent would greet him cordially and ask about Lorraine and the child. Then they would go to the house on the corner, and over a glass of wine, Tony would explain just how he happened to be short and talk about his plans for the future. The meeting usually ended with Kent taking him to a local Italian restaurant for dinner, with Tony eating voraciously and silently as Kent toyed with his food and talked. Tony was no conversationalist, and left Kent with the feeling that he was talking to himself. His need for friendship, companionship, someone to talk to, was acute and was not satisfied until he made friends with Thorvald Miller.

Chapter 15

IT was after eight o'clock when Rabbi Small, in phylacteries and prayer shawl, recited the morning prayers. He was at home in his study, facing east, of course. He had overslept and so was too late to go to the minyan, which began at seven. As he began the *Shimon Esrai* prayer, his meditation was suddenly disturbed by the racket of the peripatetic gardener mowing the lawn of the house across the street. By an effort of will, he finished the morning prayers, and then, after doffing and folding his prayer shawl and replacing it in its blue velvet bag, and winding up the leather straps of his phylacteries, he repaired to the breakfast nook, which adjoined the kitchen.

Miriam had already eaten. Now she served his breakfast of eggs and toast, poured his coffee, and then filled her own cup again and sat down opposite him. She could see that he was annoyed by the noise outside, and said, "It doesn't last long; only while he's doing their front lawn. When he goes around to the back, you can still hear him, but it's not too bad."

"I wonder if you realize how much this place has changed since we first came twenty-five years ago," he said. "Back then people used hand mowers, and the snick-snick of the blade as they walked up and down their lawns was not an unpleasant sound. And when they trimmed their hedges, they used hand shears. Now it's all done by machine, and the raking is done by electric blowers. It seems as though all morning long there is the sound of grass or hedge being cut. Yesterday afternoon there was a god-awful racket—"

"That was the Rinaldos, two doors down, taking down that big tree on their front lawn that had been damaged by the storm," she said.

"Well, I remember when that used to be done with a handsaw, one of those two-man saws. The point is, it was quiet. It didn't disturb you when you wanted to read, and you didn't have to raise your voice when you wanted to talk. And the traffic—have you noticed how much traffic there is these days? Where do all the cars come from?"

"I suppose it's because a lot of those big old houses downtown and on the Point have been turned into condominiums. So where there were one or two cars, now there are a dozen. What are you getting at, David?"

He pushed his plate aside and leaned back in his chair. "I was thinking that maybe we ought to think about moving to the city—"

"And leave Barnard's Crossing?"

"What I had in mind was keeping this place for the summer, and weekends. I thought we might get a small place in Boston, a studio apartment—"

"So you wouldn't have to drive in every day?"

"There would be that, of course. But I was also thinking that it's not easy being a rabbi emeritus if you go on living in the same place after the new rabbi has arrived. I've performed three marriages since I resigned. I didn't want to, but the parents of the bride in each case were importunate. I had married them, and they wanted their daughter married by the rabbi who had married them. Although Rabbi Selig agreed—at least he raised no objections—I was uncomfortable."

"You could always refuse."

"It isn't only that. The congregation expects me to sit on the bimah in front of the Ark, along with Rabbi Selig, for the Friday evening services and the Sabbath services, for all services held upstairs in the Sanctuary. Last Friday night one of the congregants approached me at the collation in the vestry after the service to say that he'd noticed that I didn't agree with what Rabbi Selig had said in his sermon. How did he know? He'd watched me while the rabbi was talking, and he could see in my face that I took exception to the rabbi's remarks. And I couldn't budge him from his opinion. As a matter of fact, I barely heard what Rabbi Selig was saying, and after a while I stopped trying. It's not easy to hear when you're sitting behind the speaker. The microphone focuses the sound away from you. I was thinking of something else at the time."

"But we'd be leaving all our friends if we move to the city," she objected.

"What friends? We don't really have many here, you know. We were invited out a lot because I was the rabbi rather than because they liked us. And perhaps you've noticed, there's already been a falling in the number of invitations we've received. Besides, socializing is largely a weekend affair, and we'll be coming back for weekends, at least when the weather is good."

"It looks as though you've already made up your mind," she remarked.

"Oh, I wouldn't make up my mind on something like this without talking it over with you," he said quickly.

"It would make a nice change," she admitted, "but selling this house in today's market—"

"Oh, I wasn't planning on leaving Barnard's Crossing. What I had in mind was to rent just for the school year."

"And come back here for the summer?"

"And weekends."

"You mean we'd drive back here Friday afternoon and go to Boston Monday morning?"

"Or Sunday. There'd be less traffic."

"It wouldn't work, David. Your class on Friday gets through at noon. Then I suppose you sometimes have to stick around to answer questions or just to talk. It would be one o'clock before you got home and two by the time you'd had a bite of lunch and were ready to leave. I couldn't prepare for the Sabbath in that time."

"All right, so we wouldn't go back weekends. We'd just go back during the vacations, Thanksgiving and Christmas."

"You seem awfully anxious."

"Well, I really would like to get out of Selig's way. I haven't been comfortable here since he took over. And I don't suppose it's too pleasant for him, either. But I thought I'd just have to suffer through it. And then Mordecai Jacobs—you remember him, the fellow who is going to marry the Lerner girl—he lives in an apartment house near Coolidge Corner. He said quite a few of the tenants go to Florida for the winter, and some of them are willing to rent their apartments while they're gone. Well, yesterday he told me that he spoke to someone whose apartment was just below his, and when he told him he knew a rabbi who might be interested in taking their place for the winter, they were pretty eager. See, they're observant, and if a rabbi took their apartment, they wouldn't have to put away their dishes and silverware."

"When can we see it?"

"Any morning, according to Jacobs. Today, if you like."

"I'll get dressed."

Chapter 16

"WE'LL move Friday morning," the rabbi announced.

"Why Friday?" asked Miriam. "Why not Sunday as we originally planned?"

"Because if we're here Friday, we'll have to go to the evening services, and that means that I'd have to sit up in front beside the Ark with Rabbi Selig, and then go down with him to the vestry for the collation. Each time it has led to some embarrassment for both of us. I'd just as soon skip it."

"All right, then I'd better start packing."

"What is there to pack? Just take the dresses and stuff you'll need for the next week or two."

"But dishes, pots and pans—"

"We don't need them, Miriam. The Rosenblooms keep a kosher kitchen."

"But if I just take a few dresses—what if something comes up and there's a particular dress I'd need for the occasion—"

"So we can always drive out here on a Sunday morning."

On Thursday, at the morning minyan, in casual conversation with Rabbi Selig, he mentioned that he would be moving to Boston the next morning. He thought his younger counterpart appeared pleased, although he said, "I'll miss your presence here in Barnard's Crossing, Rabbi. I always felt more secure knowing I could count on your experience with the town, with the congregation."

"Well, I won't be far away, and I'll be coming back from time to time."

Friday morning, the rabbi again said his morning prayers at home. Then after a leisurely breakfast, they loaded the car with the clothes they might need in the next couple of weeks and started out. As usual, she was careful not to talk to him while he was driving, but when they arrived at their new home on Beacon Street, she said, "You were driving kind of fast at times."

"But I didn't exceed the speed limit. I tried to keep up with it. And on the Boston Road there is very little traffic at that hour."

"Well, you made it in an hour and a quarter."

"The State Road is shorter. I could have made it in an hour if I'd gone that way. But there's a lot more traffic on the State Road."

They brought up their bags and hung their clothes in the closets that had been cleared for them. "Now all I've got to do to get to the school is walk across the street and take a streetcar to Kenmore Square and walk a couple of blocks to Clark Street. And there I am, maybe a total of fifteen minutes."

"That's wonderful," she exclaimed. "Are you leaving now?"

"Might as well."

"Shall I fix you a sandwich?"

"What for? I'll be coming home for lunch. Not every day, although I could have my lunch here and then go back to school and hang around for a couple of hours. Except that once home, I'd like to stay home. But on Friday, very few classes are scheduled for the afternoon and the place is practically deserted."

As expected, he got home at half past twelve. "I thought I'd make something light for lunch, David," she said as he sat down at the kitchen table where the dishes had been set. "I thought we'd have sardines or tuna fish, or something from a can. But I went shopping and they have everything here. So I got some frozen blintzes."

"And you were able to shop for this evening?"

"No trouble. In fact, it's a lot easier than in Barnard's Crossing, and more convenient. You'll have your regular Sabbath dinner tonight."

"Good. And you had no trouble with the utensils or the stove?"

"No, everything is fine. And how was your class? Did they all come? I remember the last time you had trouble with attendance for the Friday class."

"Ah, but that was because it came in the afternoon, at one o'clock. Since this class comes before noon, they don't have to cut to get an early start to their weekend dates. I think that the fact that there are so few of us, and that we sit around a table, may have something to do with it. It makes for a feeling of responsibility. And these seem more interested in the subject. They've all attended a Religious School of some sort, and all have been confirmed or have been Bar Mitzvahed, or Bat Mitzvahed. Two of them have been to Israel. You know, I asked them to write a couple of paragraphs on their backgrounds, and every one of them turned in a paper. That's a little unusual. Usually one or two come with some excuse for not having it ready to hand in. And one, a girl, wrote a paragraph in Hebrew."

"How about this McBride woman who's auditing the course?"

"Well, naturally, she didn't."

"But she came? She's interested? You think she'll stick it out?"

"I—I think so. But I haven't been able to figure her. When she came to my office Tuesday, she said it was to get some paper from her old desk. But I got the feeling that it was to size me up. Wednesday, she came late for the first class. She seemed distressed, but seemed all right by the end of the class when she stopped to explain why she had been late. Then yesterday when I passed her in the corridor, I said hello and she just nodded and hurried on. Then this morning, she was late again, and looked uncomfortable, but then sort of relaxed. I suppose she finds the situation strange, sitting around a table with a bunch of kids, and all of them Jewish."

"Maybe it's morning sickness," said Miriam. "Sounds like it."

"Morning sickness? You think she might be pregnant? Hmm, maybe that's why she's taking the course, so she can decide in which religion the child should be brought up."

Chapter 17

U NLIKE the regular evening service on the other days of the week, the Friday evening service began at half past eight, after dinner, rather than at seven, and instead of the usual dozen or fifteen—or when the weather was very bad, the required minimum of ten—a couple of hundred usually attended. The service was held in the sanctuary rather than in the vestry as on the rest of the week. Rabbi Selig, in an academic robe, long silk prayer shawl, and high white yarmulke, gave a short sermon, and when the service was ended, all repaired to the vestry for coffee or tea and cake. It was more social than religious, and men came with their wives and their grown sons and daughters.

The Harris brothers, Ronnie and Ben, had come without their wives. They had dined earlier, the regular Sabbath meal of gefilte fish, soup, roast chicken, at Ronnie's house. At forty-five he was six years older than his brother Ben, and more conservative in his habits, so the Sabbath meal was more often at his house.

They had all planned to go to the Friday evening service afterward, but Ronnie's wife said she was tired and would just as soon stay home, and Ben's wife thought she ought to stay and keep her company. So the two brothers had gone by themselves. And now, a little after ten, as they made their way through the parking lot to their car, Ben remarked, "The rabbi didn't look so good tonight, sort of pale."

"He caught a cold, I suppose. He sneezed a couple of times up there beside the Ark. What do you expect? You go running in this kind of weather, you're bound to catch cold."

"You don't catch cold from the weather. You get it from germs, usually in a room full of people where someone is bound to have a cold and coughs or sneezes."

"Oh yeah? So why do people get colds in winter and not in summer? And how does it look for a rabbi to be out in the street, running in short pants or those droopy sweatpants?"

"So what? That's on his own time. On the bimah he looks—"

"He looks like a cantor in the gown and with that high yarmulke."

"It's better than the way Rabbi Small used to look up there in the wrinkled suit and the dusty shoes."

"Rabbi Small's shoes were dusty because he always walked to the temple. He wouldn't ride on the Sabbath," said Ronnie severely.

"Well, he could have wiped them before he came on the bimah."

"Probably never occurred to him. See, he was a rabbi all the time, twenty-four hours a day; not just when he was giving a sermon."

"Yeah, well, you got to admit the kids like Rabbi Selig. He plays basketball with them."

"Well, when my kids were going to Hebrew School, they liked Rabbi Small. And do you know why? Not because he played with them, but because he talked to them as though they were adults. And they appreciated it."

"Seems to me," said Ben, "you were not too crazy about Small when he was here."

"Maybe, but that was because he was a kind of cold fish. I

mean, I didn't care for him personally, but I couldn't fault him as a rabbi. Now, Rabbi Selig, he's a nice, friendly kind of guy. If he were my accountant, or my doctor, or if I were doing business with him, he'd be fine, just fine. But as my rabbi . . . Look here, his closest friend here in Barnard's Crossing is that lawyer Lew Baumgold, who isn't a member of the temple, and who doesn't go to services even on the High Holidays. And what's more, he's married to a *shiksa*."

"He's friendly with Lew because they jog together. And as for that *shiksa*, she teaches at Windermere. And what's more, she's pretty friendly with Rabbi Small; takes his course in Judaic Philosophy. I got that from Cy Kaplan, whose son goes there."

"No kidding! Maybe she's planning to convert."

"Could be. And maybe that's why Rabbi Selig is so friendly with Lew Baumgold."

Chapter 18

THEY took seats around three sides of the oblong table as the rabbi wheeled his armchair from behind his desk to the fourth side of the table. "I thought we might spend the hour in an informal discussion of the subject I asked you to think about, the phrase from Isaiah that Jews are to be a light unto the nations. Anyone . . ."

"Well, there's Einstein and—and Freud and—and—"

"Nah, they're just individuals who happened to be Jews," a student objected.

"And Marx, and a whole slew of others. He wouldn't've made a prophecy of individuals. He meant the whole race," said another.

"That's right, because you find smart individuals in all races. It's ideas he meant, not the accomplishment of some one person."

The rabbi nodded approvingly. "And these ideas would have to be ideas that all Jews held, or were generally accepted and lived by," said the rabbi. "But they'd also have to be ideas that other nations have come to accept, or the light wouldn't be any use to them. Isn't that right?"

"Sure, a light's no use if you're blind."

"Or blindfolded."

"Or looking the other way."

"So what ideas did the Jews develop that the other nations accepted?"

"Well, the idea of one God, monotheism," a student suggested.

"Yeah, but the Christians and the Muslims, too, have monotheism," another objected.

"But they got it from us."

"So that shows that they saw the light."

"And what was the advantage of monotheism?" asked the rabbi. "The assumption is that light is better than darkness, so what did the other nations gain by this bit of light?"

"Where there's more than one, they can disagree."

"Sure, you see it in Homer, in the *Iliad*, where the gods are on different sides."

"One god is like a referee or an umpire. So a thing is right or it's wrong. With one God you have justice."

"Very good," said the rabbi. "Is there anything else?"

"How about the Sabbath?"

"What about it?"

"Well, it sort of established a day of rest. For Christians it's Sunday, and for Muslims it's Friday, but didn't we establish the general principle?"

The rabbi rose from his chair and said, "Why don't I list these on the blackboard." Then he wrote down "Monotheism." Under it, he wrote "Sabbath." "Anything else?" he asked.

"We don't hunt and shoot animals for pleasure, and a lot of people are beginning to feel the same way."

"We don't even shoot them for food. They'd be *traif*."

"There's a movement against fox hunting in England."

"Yeah, and how about the whales?"

"All right," the rabbi said, and wrote down "Animals." "It's more than just not shooting them," he added. "We avoid hurting them. We don't yoke a donkey and an ox together. We do not muzzle the ox that treads the corn. We do not take eggs from a nest if the mother bird is watching."

"Labor," someone called out.

"What about labor?"

"You've got to pay labor the prevailing wage, and they can organize in a union."

"And they have to be paid in cash; no company store."

"How about literacy? Don't we equate the degree of civilization with the degree of literacy? And we've been a hundred percent literate for a couple of thousand years."

"Cleanliness; washing your hands before eating. I read somewhere that in the Middle Ages dirt was a mark of holiness."

"Enjoyment; we're supposed to enjoy ourselves."

When the bell rang, signaling the end of the hour, they did not rush out as they normally would, but got up from their seats slowly, still continuing to discuss among themselves the subject matter of the class. Sarah McBride lingered on, and when they had all left, she asked in response to the rabbi's inquiring look, "How do you go about converting?"

"The discussion in class—"

She shook her head. "I've been thinking about it for some time."

"We don't proselytize, in part because it used to be forbidden and in part because it wasn't necessary; the righteous Gentile had the same standing with us as the observant Jew."

"I wasn't thinking of myself," she said. "But if I have a child, I figure it will be a lot easier to bring up if both parents have the same religion."

The rabbi nodded. "I see. Well, with us conversion is primarily adoption, adoption into the tribe. It isn't just changing your mind about what you believe. See, we made a compact with God, a real contract binding Him and us. So the convert has to be one of us; not merely someone who thinks the way we do. It involves a change of name, for one thing. Usually Abraham for a man and Sarah for a woman." He smiled. "But your name is Sarah, so you're already halfway there."

"That's all there is to it? A change of name?"

"Oh no. There are conversion classes, which involve a course of study, for about six months, I think. Then there is an examination, and finally circumcision for the man and a kind of ritual bath for the woman."

"Would this course that I'm taking with you be the equivalent of the conversion class?"

The rabbi shook his head. "No, conversion classes are quite different; they deal with the actual practice, the observance of the commandments, the holidays and how they are to be kept. It's quite different from what I intend for this course. When you take a conversion class, you are apt to end up knowing a lot more about the practice of the religion than your Jewish partner."

"Then . . ." She spread her arms in questioning dejection.

"Unless he takes the class along with you. It's not unusual."

"I don't get it. If he doesn't know any more about it than I do, and a lot less than I'll know after taking a six-month course—"

"I've never met your husband, but from what little you've said, I know quite a bit about him. He grew up in an observant family, I gather from what you said about his eating habits. I suspect he's a practicing Jew although not an observant one. His thinking is quite different from yours. You said you felt you had sinned when you had an evil thought and that you would list it among your sins when you went to Confession, and do penance for it. He didn't feel he had sinned unless he had actually done something wrong to a person; it would never occur to him that he could gain forgiveness through prayer or penance, but only from the person he had wronged.

"He's not afraid of hell, and he doesn't look forward to an eternity in Heaven when he dies. Faith, which is so important to you, has little meaning for him. He may or may not believe in the existence of God, but if as a result of reading some philosophical work, say, he decided he's an atheist, it wouldn't affect his behavior in the least."

He nodded at the blackboard. "Think of some of the things that were mentioned in class; literacy, for one. If his child showed no interest in his schoolwork, it would bother him a lot. And if he dropped out of school, he would regard it as a tragedy. These are Jewish attitudes that he absorbed in the same way that he absorbed his food habits."

"But I'd feel the same way if a child of mine dropped out of school, or couldn't read."

"But would your great-great-grandfather have felt that way, or would he have thought that reading was a function of the local priest?"

"All right. You're saying that we got it from you. That's what you mean by Israel being a light unto the nations. Okay. Whether we got them from you, or came to them on our own, what difference does it make? Our attitudes are the same now."

"No, no, no," said the rabbi, shaking his head. "They're quite different. You pray, which means to beg, to entreat. We *daven.* The origin of the word is obscure, but it consists of giving thanks for blessings we receive. It's simplistic, but where you say, 'Give us this day our daily bread,' we say, 'Blessed art thou, O Lord, who brought forth bread from the earth.' We call it praying for lack of a better word, and because outwardly it resembles what you do.

"Charity. We both consider it important. But you give out of the goodness of your heart, whereas with us it's a sort of tax that we're shamed or constrained into giving. Even when we use our traditional terms, you tend to equate them to something in your religion that is actually quite different. A synagogue is not the equivalent of a church, and a rabbi is not at all like your priest or minister. As a rabbi, I am a purely secular figure with no liturgical function whatsoever. I am a rabbi by virtue of having studied our Law, passed an examination, and been declared capable of sitting as a judge in cases brought before me. I don't bless people or things. Periodically the Kohanim, the descendants of Aaron, who frequently have names like Cohen or Kahn or Katz or Kagan, bless the congregation."

"And my Lew knows all this stuff because his folks kept a kosher house?"

"I'm sure he's aware of the difference in the way he's asked for a contribution to the Red Cross from the way he's approached to contribute to the UJA. And having been in a synagogue, I'm sure he realizes that the rabbi has no liturgical function. If he's ever been in a church, then he must have noticed the difference between your praying and our *davening*. Yes, I'm sure he's aware of much of what I told you."

"Then maybe I ought to talk to him about this conversion class. Maybe I could get him to go with me. You see, I'm going to have a baby."

"Oh, congratulations. When do you expect—"

"To give birth? Sometime in May or early June."

Curiously, as the rabbi made his way home, the thought uppermost in his mind was that he could tell Miriam that she had guessed right.

Chapter 19

WHILE for Rabbi Small the convenience of being a short streetcar ride from the college was an improvement over driving to and from Barnard's Crossing, the move to Brookline opened up a whole new world for Miriam. Since she did not drive, she had been dependent on the rabbi, always a reluctant driver, or friends who happened to be going where she wanted to go, or the bus, which ran once an hour. But now she could go into the city with all its wonders by just walking across the street and taking a streetcar, which came by every few minutes.

However, they did not lose touch with Barnard's Crossing. Al Bergson would call at least once a week to report anything of interest that may have happened at the temple. His wife called Miriam almost daily and would come into the city occasionally to meet with her for a shopping expedition, or to visit the museum, or to attend a concert. On one occasion, Chief Lanigan, having business in the city, stopped off at the college late in the afternoon, and the rabbi persuaded him to come home with him for dinner. He stayed a couple of hours afterward, regaling them with news of the town, of actions taken by the Board of Selectmen and the School Committee, and of incidents that the police had had to deal with.

It was on a Sunday morning that Miriam declared, "David, I haven't got a thing to wear. I simply have to get some more clothes."

"No problem," he replied. "We'll drive out to Barnard's Crossing today and you can get your fall and winter things and bring back what you won't be using. As a matter of fact, I've got to get some books."

"Shall we call the Bergsons and tell them we're coming?"

"No-o, I think we better not. They're bound to ask us to come over for tea, and by the time we leave, it will be getting dark."

"But what if they see us—"

"Oh, we can say it was a spur-of-the-moment thing, that we had gone out for a drive and just happened to come this way."

"All right," she said doubtfully.

They started out shortly after lunch and arrived in Barnard's Crossing around two o'clock. The rabbi drove into the garage and they entered the house through the breezeway and the back door. They had almost finished loading the car with things they needed when the doorbell rang. It was Al Bergson.

"Ben Halprin said he saw a car in the garage, so I came over to check."

"Well—"

"I thought it might be somebody breaking in because I was sure that if you were coming here, you would have given me a call."

"I tried to," said the rabbi, "but the line was busy."

"That's the missus, of course."

"So I thought if we got through here early, we'd drop by and surprise you."

"You finished here? So come on along."

"We can't stay long," said the rabbi. "I don't want to drive back in the dark."

"Well, come and have a cup of coffee. Edie baked a strudel that's out of this world."

As they sipped their coffee and munched strudel, Edith Bergson said, "You know, I thought you folks would be coming out weekends. Don't you miss Barnard's Crossing?"

"Oh, we do," said the rabbi, "but weekends are difficult. If we were to start out Friday, it would be too late for Miriam to prepare for the Sabbath. And on Saturday, I don't drive until after sunset, and that means driving in the dark, which I tend to avoid. So we could come out Sunday, stay overnight, and drive back Monday morning, but the last few Sundays have been rainy, and we've got in the habit of just lazing around and reading the Sunday papers."

"But Thanksgiving, there's no school on Friday. So that's four days. You'll be coming out Thanksgiving, won't you?"

"Yes, we planned to."

"Good, then we'll expect you for Thanksgiving dinner," said Edith with an air of finality that brooked no opposition.

By the time they left, it was growing dark. Miriam was careful not to speak as they rode since he was always tense at the wheel of the car and doubly so when he had to drive at night. But when they were back in the apartment and had put away the things they had brought, she said, "You not only made up a fib, but then you changed it to another, and in the end it didn't work. We had to go over to the Bergsons' and drive home at night."

"Yes," he said, "I suppose that's how fibs work out."

"And how did you know Edith would be on the phone?"

"I didn't, and Al didn't. We both just assumed it."

She laughed. "Well, at least we've got Thanksgiving taken care of."

Chapter 20

ALTHOUGH it had been cloudy all day, it did not begin to
rain until after nightfall, around five o'clock, when Susan Selig returned home from her bar review course in Salem. The rabbi was
at the temple, and she presumed he would be there for about another hour. Unlike the bar review she had taken in Connecticut
years before, in which the class had consisted of almost a hundred and been confined to lectures, this one in Salem had only
about a dozen and entailed some discussion. She had got involved in an argument with a young fellow who had just graduated from law school, and she had come out second best. As a
result she was a little out of sorts. And tired.

Since they were going to dine on yesterday's roast, which she
had only to reheat, she decided to wait until her husband got
home before preparing dinner. She went into the bedroom, sat
down on the bed, and kicked off her shoes. Then she laid back
her head on the pillow. After a while, she decided to get into
nightgown and robe to be really comfortable, and loll about until
her husband got home.

Although the house was isolated with no other house on the
bedroom side for a couple of hundred yards, she pulled the

shade down because she had lived in apartment houses most of her life, and it was automatic with her.

The rain had grown heavier, and then there was a sudden cloudburst and a flash of lightning; and she saw in the inch or so at the bottom of the shade, a pair of eyes peering in at her.

Curiously calm, she went to the hall where the telephone was, and dialed 911.

Her call was answered almost immediately. "Sergeant Riordan."

"This is Susan Selig—"

"The rabbi's wife?"

"That's right."

"What can I do for you, Mrs. Selig?"

"There's someone on the porch looking in at my bedroom."

"Are you alone?"

"Yes."

"The patrol car is in your neighborhood, ma'am. I know the address, and somebody will be there in a minute. It's right nearby. Now, don't leave your house. Just wait there, but stay out of the bedroom."

❖   ❖   ❖

Professor Kent quickly scrambled to his feet from his kneeling position as he heard the car coming up the driveway. Squinting in the glare of the patrol car's headlights, he said, "I was on my way to my friends the Millers, on Evans Road, and I took shelter from the storm on the porch here."

Sergeant Aherne had got out of the car. He ran his flashlight up and down the figure in front of him and focused the light on his knees, which showed the dust of the porch. "And you knelt to give thanks for your delivery from the rain?"

Professor Kent chuckled uneasily. "No, Officer, I thought I

heard a sound, er—like a scream, maybe, so I knelt to see if some-one was in trouble."

Aherne walked back to the patrol car to confer with his col-league behind the wheel. Then he motioned with his flashlight to Kent. "You going to the Millers'? All right, get in."

"Oh, thank you. Thank you very much," Kent said, and got in the backseat.

Aherne walked around to the front of the house and rang the bell. Mrs. Selig, in a dressing gown, opened the door but kept it on the chain.

"Sergeant Aherne, ma'am. We have the man in the patrol car. He says he was going to the Millers' on Evans Road. That he took shelter on your porch from the cloudburst. He says he heard a scream and that's why he tried to look in, to see if anyone was in trouble. Did you have your radio or TV on?"

"No. Neither was on."

"Yeah, like I figured. The rabbi at the temple?"

"Unless he had to go see someone."

"But you expect him home pretty soon?"

She glanced at her watch. "He should be along any minute."

"We could wait here a few minutes," he offered.

"Oh, I don't think that's necessary. I don't suppose there was anyone else with him."

"All right then, but if your husband is delayed and you feel un-easy, I could call in and have a policeman come down and wait around until he gets home."

"Oh, that's very kind of you, Sergeant, but really, I don't think it will be necessary."

"Okay, but if you change your mind, just let us know."

In the car, Kent felt it necessary to make conversation. "I am Professor Kent, and Professor Thorvald Miller is my colleague on the faculty of Windermere College. I come here frequently for the weekend. My wife's people used to own this land. In fact, they built the house where—where I took shelter, and the Miller house, too. So I felt as though I were coming home, you know." He chuckled. "Which is why I chose to walk up the house side of the hedge. The other side, the right-of-way, is apt to be muddy when it rains. Ah, here we are. Very kind of you to give me a lift. I'll—"

"Just sit there awhile," said Aherne as he got out and mounted the steps of the porch to the front door. He rang the bell, and when Professor Miller appeared, he asked, "You expecting someone tonight?"

"Why—I—"

But Kent called out through the open car door, "It's me, Thorvald. The police gave me a lift."

"Oh, yes. It's Professor Kent. Yes, we're expecting him."

Aherne returned to the car and opened the rear door. He waited until Kent had mounted the porch steps and entered the house. Then he took his seat in the car, and as his colleague set it in motion, he asked, "You believe any of that, the guy using the house side of the hedge because the other side might be muddy, and taking shelter on the porch because of the rain, and kneeling because he thought he heard a scream?"

"Nah."

"Neither do I."

"The other side of the hedge got flagstones and is no more muddy than the house side."

"I know. So why didn't you squeeze him a little?"

"I would've, but where it was the rabbi's wife that was involved, it could make for a lot of trouble."

Chapter 21

"**A**NYTHING?" Chief Lanigan asked of the desk sergeant as he made his way to his office.

"There was a Peeping Tom call from the rabbi's wife."

"Miriam Small reported a Peeping Tom?"

"No, the new rabbi, Rabbi Selig. Mrs. Selig called to say she was in her bedroom and she thought she saw someone looking at her through the inch or so below the drawn blind. I notified the cruiser and Tim Aherne caught the fellow. He said he was going to the Millers' on Evans Road, so Tim took him there."

"Where is Aherne now?"

"Up by the wharf. He'll be off in about a half an hour."

"All right, tell him I want to see him when he comes in."

Lanigan headed for his office. Then stopped. "If you've got Peeping Tom on your blotter, change it to trespass."

"Why?"

"Because when it appears in the newspaper that the rabbi's wife reported a Peeping Tom, it can cause some trouble."

"I don't get it, Chief."

"No? What if it were a nun who reported it?"

The desk sergeant, who like Lanigan was Catholic, nodded slowly. "Yeah, I see what you mean."

Later, when Aherne appeared before him, Lanigan asked him to recount the incident, and then said, "You're sure he was kneeling? Did you see him kneeling?"

"No-o. He must've got up when he saw our headlights coming up the driveway. But when I flashed the spot on him, he was brushing the dust off his pants."

"And you took him to the Millers'?"

"That's right. I wasn't giving him a lift, you know. I wanted to see if they were expecting him."

"And they were?"

"I guess so. But before I had a chance to ask them, he yelled out from the cruiser."

"I see. And the rabbi's wife, was she upset?"

"Not that I could see. I offered to have a man wait there until her husband got home, but she said it wasn't necessary, and that her husband was due home almost any minute."

Lanigan leaned back in his armchair. "The Millers, you know anything about them?"

"He's a teacher, in Boston, I think."

"I know that. He's not married, but his mother lives with him and keeps house for him. You haven't heard anything about her, have you?"

Aherne shook his head. "Ada Bronson works for her; she might know something."

"Ada Bronson? Jimmie Bronson's wife?"

"That's right. Not regular, I understand. She goes there every now and then to help out. Wednesdays mostly, Jimmie said, to help her clean up and to keep her company on account her son gets home late on Wednesdays."

"Just two of them, I shouldn't think they'd need much in the way of help."

"Yeah, but the old lady is not well. Got asthma pretty bad. Sometimes she just lays in bed or on the divan in the living room and Ada does all the work, makes the supper and everything."

"How old would you say she was?"

"You mean the Miller woman?" A shrug of the shoulders. "Sixty, sixty-five."

"And this fellow you caught?"

"You mean the Peeping Tom? He looks about the same age, maybe sixty-five or seventy."

"So he might be visiting the old lady rather than the son."

"Yeah, I guess he could be."

"Maybe I'll drop in and visit the Millers. Who was on the cruiser with you?"

"Bob Slocumbe."

"Okay. Look, it's on the blotter as a trespass. Understand?"

"Sure, Chief."

"So tell Slocumbe."

"Okay."

Chapter 22

RABBI Selig came home about ten minutes after the departure of the police. As happens in New England, the weather had cleared and the moon was bright in the cloudless sky. He parked his car in the garage and came in through the back door to the kitchen. When he saw that his wife was in nightgown and robe, he asked, "Don't you feel well?"

"Oh, I feel all right. Why do you ask?"

"Well, you don't usually get into nightgown and robe this early in the evening."

"I was kind of headachy after the bar review and I thought I'd feel better if I lay down for a while, but . . ."

"But what?"

"Oh, Dana." Her eyes filled with tears, and she told him what had happened.

"I'm going over there right now and—"

"Oh, please don't, Dana. Not now. You might get into a fight." She managed a smile through her tears. "And there'd be all kinds of trouble if it got out. You might get a black eye, and how would it look? And what would the congregation think of their rabbi with a black eye? Wait until you've quieted down a little."

"All right, I'll see him tomorrow."

He debated whether to go to the police first to get their view of what had happened, and then decided that if he did, it might become public knowledge, which could be embarrassing. So the following night, after the evening service, he drove up Evans Road and parked his car in front of the Miller house.

He rang the bell, and when Miller opened the door, he said, "I am Rabbi Selig and—"

"Oh yes, my neighbor. Won't you come in?"

Reluctantly Rabbi Selig moved into the hallway.

"As the older resident, I should have called on you when you first moved in, instead of your coming to me," said Miller.

"I came about your guest last night."

"That was Professor Kent, a distinguished scholar."

"Well, I have a message for that distinguished scholar. Would you tell him that if I ever see him on my side of the hedge, I'll punch him in the nose."

Miller smiled. "Those are harsh words from a man of the cloth."

"I'm not a man of the cloth and I have no pretense to special standing with the Deity. Just tell him if I see him, I'll punch him in the nose."

"Professor Kent is an old man, about seventy, and you are, I'd say, about half that age. He weighs about a hundred and twenty-five pounds, and you are six one? Six two? You'd have a hard time explaining your fighting with a frail, old man."

"All right," said Rabbi Selig, "so I won't punch him in the nose. You just tell him, if I see him on my side, I'll pick him up bodily and toss him over the hedge. Will you tell him that?"

"Oh, I assure you, there won't be any more trouble. You see, Professor Kent's folks used to own the land from the old Boston Road clear down to Gardner's Cove, and they built this house and the one you're living in. His wife's folks, actually, so he's apt to feel that he can still go where he wants to in this area. But I made it plain to him last night that he can't do that sort of thing now. He's a frequent visitor here; it has pleasant associations for him. Normally he drives here. He likes to drive, and he's a good driver. It's a pleasant hour-or-so run for him. But last night he didn't come from home. He was downtown in Boston, so he took the bus instead of going home and picking up his car. See, he knew I'd drive him in the next morning."

"All right, but remember to tell him that if I see him on my land, I'll pick him up—" he extended his hands as though to pick up a child under the armpits "—and toss him over the hedge. Will you tell him that?"

"I'll tell him, but I assure you it won't be necessary."

Rabbi Selig nodded, and without further words, left the house and got into his car. When he got home, he greeted his wife with, "We won't be troubled again by anyone going to the Millers' over our land."

Chapter 23

WHEN Chief Lanigan called to ask if Miller was going to be home that evening, and if he was free, Mrs. Miller was pleased. "It must be they want you to serve on some town committee, Thor," she said.

"More likely he's going to try to sell me something, like tickets to the Policemen's Ball, or sign something, a petition for a wage raise, maybe."

Nevertheless, when Lanigan came, he greeted him graciously. His mother, a large, stoutish woman with puffy cheeks and protruding eyes, was effusive. When they were seated in the living room, she got up to offer their guest a plate of cookies, then some chocolates, asking each time, "You're sure you wouldn't want a cup of tea? Or coffee, perhaps? It's no trouble."

"I came because I thought we ought to get acquainted," said Lanigan.

Mrs. Miller smirked her satisfaction and gave her son an "I told you so" look.

"You see," Lanigan went on, "we're a small town, but we cover a lot of territory. In addition to the residential area, we have the responsibility for the harbor. We don't have a large police force, so we operate differently from the way they do in a city. We try to keep informed on everything that's going on. We listen and we hear a lot of gossip and rumors, and when we sense that trouble is brewing, we try to nip it in the bud. Now, the other night we got a call from your neighbor, the one whose backyard adjoins yours, that someone was peeping through her window. Our cruising car happened to be nearby, and when it was alerted by the desk sergeant, they went right over and they were able to catch the man at the window."

"That was Professor Kent," said Mrs. Miller, "a very distinguished scholar who comes from an important family."

"He took refuge from the cloudburst on their porch," said Thor Miller.

"When the officer in the cruiser focused his flashlight on him, he was busy brushing the porch dust off his pant legs," Lanigan pointed out.

"He said he thought he heard a shot and looked to see if there was trouble," Miller explained.

"There was no shot," said Lanigan.

"It may have been from the radio or the TV," said Miller.

"Neither the radio nor the TV was turned on."

"Then it could have been thunder," Miller said. "As I told the lady's husband, a Rabbi Selig, who came to complain." He went on to say. "Professor Kent's folks used to own a lot of the land here and he is still used to treating it as his own."

"And did he buy that?" asked Lanigan.

Miller shrugged, but his mother said indignantly, "He said he'd punch Professor Kent in the nose if he ever saw him on his property again. And when my son pointed out that he was an old man, he said then he'd just throw him over the hedge. Imagine a clergyman talking like that, and about a distinguished scholar like Professor Kent."

"Is he a regular visitor here?" asked Lanigan.

"He's a professor in the same college as my son is, and he's a professor, too."

"Oh, Ma!" Then to Lanigan, "He is my colleague and the senior member of my department. I feel honored that we are close. He comes here because his family used to summer here. In fact, his family built this house and the one where the rabbi lives, too. Usually he drives here, but if for some reason he takes the bus, then he'll stay overnight and drive in with me the next morning. In fact, I guess he usually stays the night."

"And when he takes the bus, he gets off at the stop in front of the rabbi's driveway?"

"That's right. I was told that there is a right-of-way from the old Boston Road clear to Gardner's Cove."

"We-el, there is a right-of-way, but it's on the other side of the hedge. I suggest that you tell your friend that if he uses the bus, he should get off at the next stop where the old Boston Road is joined by Evans Road."

"But that means a long walk," Mrs. Miller protested.

"But it could be a lot less trouble," said Lanigan. "Next time the police in the cruiser might arrest him and he'd have to spend the night in our jail instead of your guest room."

Chapter 24

NOVEMBER had been cold and rainy for much of the month, with appreciable amounts of snow in the higher elevations of New England and with the ski slopes of northern New England already sufficiently covered so that snow-making machines were needed for only the occasional bald spots. There had even been snow in the western and middle portions of the state, which the coastal area had escaped, the weather experts on the news broadcasts had explained, because of its proximity to the warmer water of the ocean.

The rabbi and Miriam had planned to drive out early in the afternoon on the Wednesday before Thanksgiving, spend the evening and night in their house in Barnard's Crossing, and then the next day walk or drive to the Bergsons' for dinner as they had promised. But Tuesday night the weather forecaster, with sweeping arm motions to illustrate the path of the jet stream, had suggested the possibility of a northeaster of possible blizzard proportions, and when the rabbi started out at ten o'clock to go to the college, snow was already falling.

"If this keeps up, we'll have to change our plans," he said to Miriam.

"Oh, it will probably stop soon, David. See, it's not sticking. But you'd better wear your rubbers anyway."

By the time he got to Kenmore Square, where he left the streetcar and walked a couple of blocks to the school, the snow was sticking and there was an inch or more on the sidewalk. The wind had also picked up considerably and he had to lean forward, clutching his hat.

❖ ❖ ❖

As he thrust his arms through the sleeves of his overcoat, a thought occurred to Lew Baumgold, and he reached for the phone. "Sarah? Lew. Look, sweetheart, I've got to be in Boston most of the day. So how about if I pick you up when I'm through, and we can go out to Barnard's Crossing together?"

"I've got a three-o'clock, Lew."

"That's even better. I won't be through until around four, so say I come down to the school at four-thirty. You get through at four, so you'll wait around in the English office for a half hour at the most."

"All right. You're sure you don't want to have Thanksgiving dinner here in Boston?"

"Sweetheart." His tone showed his exasperation. "I told you we're having dinner with Bob and Louise, and he's made reservations at Salem House."

"Oh yeah. All right, so you'll pick me up at the English office around half past four."

"Love you." And he hung up.

His partner, Jack Colby, came into the room. "Just listening to the radio," he said. "They're predicting a real nor'easter for this afternoon. If I were you, I'd go in by train or bus. You're apt to have trouble finding a parking place if there's any snow. And if you find a parking place on the street, you could find yourself plowed in if there's lots of snow."

Lew looked out the window at the street, which was already white. "Yeah, I think you're right. You got a bus schedule?"

❖   ❖   ❖

Thorvald Miller backed out of his garage and turned on his windshield wipers against the falling snow. He noted that the blade on the passenger side was not working properly: it was streaking rather than wiping clean. He turned off the motor and got out and fiddled with the spring that pressed the blade against the glass. He got back into the car and switched on the wipers again. This time, while the wiper on the driver's side seemed to work normally, the other tended to stick and move only sporadically. It occurred to him that if the snow continued, as seemed likely, it might be dangerous to drive all the way into the city, so he drove instead to nearby Swampscott station.

There, all parking spaces were taken except one of those reserved for the handicapped right next to the stairs leading to the platform. The Reserved sign was lightly covered with snow, and he reflected that if he were ticketed for using the space, he could claim that the sign had not been visible.

❖   ❖   ❖

Only two showed up at eleven o'clock for his class. "They've probably been delayed by the storm," said the rabbi. "We'll wait a few minutes."

"They won't show up," said one of the students. "They're all from out of town and made an early start for home."

"And you?"

"Oh, I'm from Newton."

"And I came from Brookline."

"All right," said the rabbi, "so we'll call it a day and you can make an early start, too." He turned to Sarah McBride and asked, "You through for the day, too?"

"Oh no, I have a three-o'clock."

"Would the cafeteria be open now? Would you care for a cup of coffee?"

"It is and I would."

As they walked to the cafeteria, she explained, "Most of the students are local and they don't cut class the day before a vacation. They certainly won't in my three-o'clock because most of them are teachers from local schools. You just happened to get a majority of out-of-towners, several from New York and at least one I know about who is from New Jersey."

"So the late-afternoon classes are well attended?"

"Usually. Professor Kent always holds an important quiz on that day to make sure they don't cut. He has a four-o'clock today."

They reached the cafeteria and got their cups of coffee. "He might cut this class, though," she went on. "He's got a big party on tonight up in Breverton. He's been boasting about it all week. It's a wedding reception at the country club there, and the bride is a Leverett."

"Indeed! And she's having it at the Breverton Country Club? I didn't realize it was that fashionable a place."

"It isn't. But she's from the poor branch of the Leveretts, the North Shore Leveretts. When they got off the *Mayflower* they went in for farming, on the North Shore of all places. The other Leveretts settled in and around Boston and went in for business and shipping."

"I see. And are you going to the North Shore for Thanksgiving, or is your husband coming into Boston?"

"Oh, I guess I'll go to Barnard's Crossing. Lew is in town on business today and I'll probably drive back with him. He said he'd stop by the English office around four when he gets through. If you're around, come up to the English office; I'd like you to meet him."

"I'm afraid not," said the rabbi. "I'm starting out for home right now."

❖ ❖ ❖

As the rabbi made his way to Kenmore station, it seemed to him that the snow was falling faster and the wind had picked up considerably. Although much of the sidewalk had been cleared in front of the stores that lined his route, he was glad that he had worn his rubbers, and when he had to cross a street and had to climb over the mounds that the snowplows had piled up, he wished that he had worn overshoes.

The plows were out in full force and Assistant Professor Morris, a new man, watched gloomily from the window of the English office as one of them came lumbering down Clark Street.

"I'm plowed in," he announced.

Professor Sugrue, head of the department, came and stood beside him.

"I'm sure you can get one of the janitors to shovel you out," he said.

"Maybe. But even if I did get shoveled out, where would I park?"

"You've got a point there," Sugrue admitted. "So how will you get home?"

"Oh, that's no problem; I'll take the streetcar."

❖ ❖ ❖

In Barnard's Crossing, Rabbi Selig looked out at the white expanse and thought that at last he was going to get a chance to use the snowblower. His wife had put on her fur coat and was now pulling on her gloves.

"You're not going to your class today, are you?"

"And whyever not?"

"Well, you'll have no trouble getting out to the road because it's been plowed, but where will you park when you get there?"

"Where I always park, in the garage half a block away. It's an important class; we're just finishing torts."

He watched her maneuver her car down the slope of their driveway and then he donned his mackinaw and went out into the garage. He rubbed his hands as he approached the snowblower. He wheeled it out of the corner where it was kept, to the open door. Then, grasping the wooden handle on the starter rope, he pulled. The engine did not start, but it gave an encouraging cough. He rewound the rope and tried again. The third time the engine started and he listened to its drumroll as he might to a favorite symphony. He pushed the blower out of the garage and into the snow, and he glowed with pleasure and a kind of pride as he saw the white arc of snow that the blower threw up.

The town plow, which had cleared half the road when Susan Selig had driven off, had by this time returned to do the other half and had sealed off the driveway, but Rabbi Selig pushed his blower into the mound, and although he had to pull back and push forward several times, he was able to clear the driveway to the road. When he had cleared a path a car-width wide, he stopped to rest and realized that his hands and face were freezing, so he wheeled the blower back into the garage, satisfied that Susan would have no trouble coming up the driveway when she came home.

❖   ❖   ❖

Professor Miller's three-o'clock class was used to getting out early on Wednesdays, and this Wednesday he did not disappoint them; he ended the class a good twenty minutes before the hour. He hurried to the English office to get his things. Professor Kent was there awaiting him.

"Oh, there you are, Thorvald. I canceled my four-o'clock. I've got to change for this formal affair up in Breverton, so if you'll hang around for a while, you can drive me up to Barnard's Crossing and—"

"I came in by train and I'll be going home by train."

"We can use my car, dear boy."

"Yes, but I have an appointment that I—I can't break."

"Oh, of course. It's Wednesday and you have an appointment every Wednesday afternoon. And what time do you expect to get home?"

"I don't know," said Miller as he edged toward the door. "Six or half past."

"Then perhaps I'll drive up myself. The radio report a little while ago said the main roads have been cleared. Perhaps I'll stop off at your place and visit with your good mother for a while. Then when you get home, you can whisk me up to Breverton in my car, take it back home with you, and then pick me up when the party is over. You can come over for a minute, to do my tie, can't you?"

"Well, just for a minute."

❖   ❖   ❖

The phone rang in the Small apartment, and the rabbi answered. It was Bergson, who said, "Look, David, the roads are clear, but I'm guessing that you're reluctant to drive out tomorrow."

"That's right."

"The radio reports the State Road is clear, but plan on taking the train. You let me know which train and I'll meet you at the station. Okay?"

"Fine. I'll call you tomorrow morning."

"By the way, David, we've invited the Seligs, too. Is that all right with you? I mean it will present no problem? You're on good terms with them?"

"Oh, sure. I look forward to seeing them."

❖　❖　❖

When Sarah McBride entered the English office at a few minutes before four, Professor Miller was obviously on the point of leaving. The phone rang and he picked it up. "For you," he said, and handed her the receiver.

It was Lew. "Look, sweetheart, I've got to be here for another half hour or so, maybe an hour, so I'll pick you up at your apartment."

"Maybe I could come and meet you. Are you at the courthouse?"

"No, I'm at the Lawyers' Building on Cornhill."

"Where are you parked?"

"I didn't drive in. I took the bus. We'll have to take the bus home."

"You're almost three blocks from the bus stop in Barnard's Crossing, and the snow must be a foot high there," she objected.

"Yeah, and they're not likely to have plowed Endicott. Look, we could take the train and get a cab at Swampscott station."

"The last time we took the train to Swampscott, we had to hang around for a half hour or more waiting for the cab we called."

"You're right. Look, why don't you go on home. Then tomorrow morning, you call me and tell me what train you can come in on and I'll pick you up at Swampscott."

"Yes, I think that'll be better."

"Love you."

❖　❖　❖

When Professor Kent opened the door in response to Professor Miller's ring, he was shaved, had bathed, and was fully dressed except that the ends of his bow tie hung down on his shirt. Professor Miller surveyed him and said, "Very nice. I've only got a couple of minutes. I should think you'd at least try to tie your tie. What if I couldn't make it?"

"It's this tendinitis in my left shoulder," said Kent. "I can't raise my arm, and when the weather is bad as it is today, I can barely raise it above my waist. But I was sure you'd come by."

"All right, turn around."

Kent turned and faced the oval mirror on the wall, and Miller crossed the ends of the tie, pulling them tight.

"A-a-rgh!"

"A bit tight, is it?" asked Miller. "All right, I'll loosen it a little." He made a loop of one end, and then pulled the other end through to make the second loop. "Now, how's that? That's a pretty good bow if I do say so myself."

Professor Kent nodded.

It was five o'clock when Susan Selig called her husband. "We're having a short break," she announced, "and we shall be finishing torts. We always have a little party when we finish a section, and it's my turn. Nothing elaborate, just coffee and doughnuts. So is the driveway cleared?"

"I cleared it right after you left."

"But a lot of snow has fallen since."

"So I'll run over it again. Er—how many of you will there be?"

"About a dozen. Why?"

"I mean, how many cars?"

"Oh, five or six. Maybe as many as eight."

"Then I'd better clear the whole terrace."

"It's not too much work, is it, dear?"

"No, I enjoy it."

He hung up and went out to sample the air. It seemed even

colder than it had been when he first plowed. He came back in, and this time he hunted about and found a stocking hat and mittens and a woolen scarf to wind around his neck under his mackinaw.

❖   ❖   ❖

Professor Miller found an empty phone booth and dialed his home. To the answering hello, he said, "Ma?"

"No, this is Ada Bronson, Professor. Your ma is lying down."

"Is she all right?"

"Oh, sure, she's just resting."

"Is Professor Kent there?"

"Professor Kent? No, there's no one here except your ma and me."

"Did he phone?"

"Not since I been here. I came at noon."

"Then I guess he decided to go straight to Breverton. I'm taking the train home. I didn't drive in today because I had trouble with my windshield wiper. I parked at Swampscott. Tell my mother I'm taking the five thirty-two, so I should be home around six."

It was almost half past five when Professor Miller was able to phone Professor Kent. It was Mrs. Bell who answered.

"Professor Kent is not here," she said. "He has a party in Breverton, so I guess he's gone there."

"Did he get someone to take him, or did he try to drive there on his own?"

"I don't know. He was gone by the time I came."

"Look, Mrs. Bell, would you take a look in the garage in back and see if his car is gone? I'll hold."

"All right." A minute or two later, she picked up the phone and said, "The car is gone, so I guess he set out on his own."

"I guess he thought I wouldn't get back to him in time. It's pretty rough out there, but the main roads appear to be clear. If he should call back, please tell him I called."

Then Professor Miller dialed his own number. Mrs. Bronson answered.

"This is Professor Miller speaking. Is my mother there?"

"She's lying down."

"Well, don't disturb her. Just tell me if Professor Kent has arrived."

"No one is here except me and the missus."

"Then I guess he went straight on to Breverton. Tell my mother I'm taking the five thirty-two and should be home a little after six."

"Yeah, you told me."

"Oh yes, I did, didn't I? Will you be there when I get home?"

"Yeah, I think the missus would like me to stay on until you come."

❖   ❖   ❖

The train was crowded and he had to stand. He did not take off his overcoat, but he placed his briefcase on the rack above his head. The train arrived at Swampscott station on time at 5:55. As usual, there was a sizable exodus, and Professor Miller hurried off with the rest. He went directly to where he had parked his car and was gratified to see that because of the overhang of the roof of the station and perhaps the wind direction, there was far less snow on his car than he had feared.

Standing beside his car, he watched the train pull out. "Damn!" he exclaimed. The man brushing the snow off the car next to his looked at him questioningly.

"I left my briefcase on the train. How long before it gets to Salem?"

The man shrugged. "Three, four minutes. I got a timetable in my car if—"

Miller shook his head. "No. I don't suppose I could get there in time."

"It will probably be in and out of Salem station before you can get your car brushed off. If you call Baggage at North station in Boston, they'll alert the conductor."

"Yeah. Guess you're right."

Arrived home, he asked his mother if Kent had called, and when she said that he had not, he said, "He's probably gone straight to Breverton. I suppose he'll call after the party."

"Is he having Thanksgiving dinner with us?"

"That was the plan, unless one of his classy friends at the party invites him."

"Well, I think he ought to let us know."

"He probably will if he thinks of it. Say, I've got to call North station. I left my briefcase on the train."

"Oh, not the one I bought you for Christmas, Thor?"

"No, not the attaché case. This is the old one with the torn strap. Look up the number, will you, Ma? I've got to have it."

❖　❖　❖

Antonio Donofrio stared gloomily out of the window of the Bixby Salon as the snow fell. The phone rang, and Lorraine, his wife, the manicurist, picked up the instrument. A moment later she called out, "Another cancellation, Tony. Mrs. Stephenson. She's the last one. She says the latest weather report is for a blizzard."

"Yeah, but according to all the earlier reports, that's for the western part of the state. Here, on the coast, they expect a couple of inches at the most. But we've been getting cancellations all day long. That's because we've got so many oldies for customers. I'll bet Hair Beautiful isn't getting any cancellations. He gets a lot of younger women, and they're not going to let a little snow keep them from looking their best on Thanksgiving. What we ought to do is aim for the young ones."

"And what do you suggest?"

"Fix the place up. Look at it. It looks like a—a barbershop. The place should be painted. We ought to have lounge chairs and magazines, and flowers, and pictures—paintings."

"That takes money, Tony."

"Not a helluvalot."

"Oh, no? Well, for your information, the bakery paid twelve hundred dollars to have their place painted. And they didn't do such a hot job."

"Okay, so say fifteen hundred. And maybe another twenty-five hundred for some new furniture. That's four thousand. That ain't much."

"And you think that will enable us to compete with Hair Beautiful? No, Tony, we'll always be at a disadvantage. That's because they're on the main street, and we're on a side street."

"So what we've got to do is advertise. And get a bigger sign. Maybe even some radio and TV advertising. On local TV, an ad would cost us what? Fifty bucks?"

"For one time. We'd have to run it every day to do any good. That's three hundred a week. Where are we going to get that kind of money?"

"From old man Kent, that's who."

"Well, I'm not asking him."

"So I'll ask him. I should think he'd be glad to do it for you. You're his only relative, he said."

"But we've borrowed from him so many times."

"Ah, a hundred, a hundred fifty, a couple hundred."

"Yes, but . . ."

"Look, if I showed him how a little loan—that's all it is,

is a loan—could make life easier for us, don't you think he'd be interested?"

Lorraine Bixby shrugged.

"Look," he urged, "it's the day before the Thanksgiving vacation. He won't be making notes, or thinking about what he'll say to his next class. He'll be free to talk to. I could invite him to come and have Thanksgiving dinner with us."

"You mean you'll drive in on a day like this?"

"No, I'll take the train in. You might need the car to do some shopping for tomorrow. I'll just walk down to the station and take the train to North station. And I can take the streetcar from there. If the trains are running, then the streetcars will be, too."

"If you think it will do any good . . ."

"What harm can it do?"

"All right. What time will you be getting home?"

"Couple of times when I went to see him in the late afternoon or early evening, he asked me to have supper with him. And then we might sit around and talk. So I could be home pretty late."

He went into the back room to change from his whites to his street clothes. She took the opportunity to open the register and remove the day's receipts, leaving only what might be needed for making change. When some minutes later, he came out in his street clothes, he strolled over to the register and pressed the Change key to open the cash drawer. He stared at the contents and then turned to her. "What happened to the money we took in this morning?"

"Oh, I deposited it," she said easily. "I didn't want it lying in the cash register over the weekend." From past experience she knew that when he ventured into Boston, he was apt to visit his buddies in the North End to gamble and maybe even fool around with girls.

He took out his wallet and riffled through the bills it contained. "Oh, well," he said, "I can always hit the old man for twenty-five or fifty if I should need it. Don't wait supper for me."

Chapter 25

THANKSGIVING Day was clear but cold, with a brisk wind that would gust every now and then, raising a cloud of powdered snow. As promised, the rabbi and Miriam were met at Swampscott by Al Bergson, sitting in his car, bundled up, the motor running to keep the heater going.

"Have you been waiting long?" asked Miriam anxiously.

"No, just got here a couple of minutes ago," said Bergson. "The trains seem to be running on time. I'll take you to your place first so that you can put up the heat. I hope you didn't shut it off."

"No, we turned the thermostat way down," said Miriam, "but we didn't shut it off."

"If you had, you might have had a pipe or two burst. I had Billy shovel off your steps and sidewalk. He was free because, of course, they called off the Barnard's Crossing–Swampscott game. Guess all games in the area were postponed or called off. Can't play where the field is covered with a foot or more of snow. Believe me, Edie was pleased even though Billy wasn't. Even when the weather is perfect, she's so nervous and fidgets until the game is over. Afraid he'll break a leg or something. Even when he is sitting on the bench, she's afraid he'll catch cold. Ah, here we are.

Not a bad job. You folks go on in and put up the thermostat. By the time you get back after dinner, your house will be nice and warm. I'll wait out here."

"Won't you come in?" asked the rabbi.

"No, David. I'm under strict orders from Edie to bring you right over. She said, 'When you bring them home to turn up the heat, don't go in because Miriam will be sure to make tea.' "

Miriam laughed. "Well, I did bring tea bags with me. All right, we'll be right out."

"You'll have something to drink, won't you, David?" Bergson suggested when they arrived at the Bergson home.

"Shouldn't we wait for the Seligs?"

"Oh, he doesn't drink anything stronger than wine, and I suspect precious little of that; just what's necessary to make *kiddush*. Probably thinks it will affect his wind or his muscles or something. He's a very health-conscious guy."

"I'll go help Edie in the kitchen," Miriam said, and left the two men to themselves.

"How's he doing?" asked the rabbi. "Getting along all right with the congregation?"

"You know how these things are: The younger men like him fine, while the older ones think it's undignified for a rabbi to be seen jogging in sweatpants, or even wearing jeans while he works around his house. And the women resent his wife not coming to Hadassah meetings or participating in the activities of the Sisterhood."

"But they knew she wouldn't when they hired him."

"Sure, but they don't have to like it. And then there was this Peeping Tom business."

"What was that all about? I didn't hear anything about a Peeping Tom."

"Your friend Lanigan listed it as trespass on the police blotter, and that's how it was reported in the press. Very decent of him.

151

But the story got out. You know how things are in a small town. Seems the rebbetzin was home alone one evening while the rabbi was at the temple. She sees someone peering in at her bedroom window through a crack under the shade. So she calls the police and the cruiser comes up and arrests this guy, who it turns out was some dirty old man who was on his way to visit Selig's neighbor on Evans Road."

"So do they think she shouldn't have called the police?"

"No, but the feeling is that if she acted like a rebbetzin, it wouldn't have happened. Ah, here are the Seligs now."

At dinner, Rabbi Selig sat beside Billy and engaged him in conversation about football, commiserating with him over the postponement of the game with their traditional rivals. He told of a game his college team had played with *their* traditional rivals and which his team had won by the Statue of Liberty play.

"What's the Statue of Liberty play?" asked Billy.

"Oh, don't you know it? The quarterback, instead of crouching over the center, stands back a couple of yards, so the opposition expects a pass. Then when the center throws the ball to him, he reaches back like he's going to throw a pass." He got up out of his chair to demonstrate the stance. "But the ends, instead of running forward to receive it, run around behind him, and one of them grabs the ball out of his hand." He resumed his seat. "See, the two ends crisscross and both act like they've each got the ball. You can only use it once in a game," said Rabbi Selig. "You try it a second time and they kill you."

Edie Bergson asked about the Small children, and Miriam explained that Hepsibah was celebrating Thanksgiving with her in-laws in Michigan and Jonathan was having dinner with his fiancée's folks.

"The same thing happened last Passover," said Rabbi Small sadly.

"Don't fret, David," said Edie Bergson. "In a few years they'll be coming back, perhaps with children."

The talk was general, about the community, the temple, and Windermere, as platters of food were passed from hand to hand. When at last coffee was served and Edie passed a plate of cookies to Rabbi Small, he shook his head and said, "I have no room, Edie. That was some meal."

"She had to make an extra effort," said Al Bergson. "She was serving two rabbis."

"There's something particularly Jewish about Thanksgiving dinner," Rabbi Small remarked. "When we *daven* we usually give thanks or we praise God for the good things He's given us. We have very few petitionary prayers, and those are usually for the people as a whole, as when we pray for rain or dew or for our return to Jerusalem. And it is sinful not to enjoy the food and the good things He offers us. We don't go in for asceticism."

"That's an interesting point," said Rabbi Selig. "Do you mind if I use it in my sermon tomorrow night?"

"It will give me pleasure if you do," said the older rabbi.

Although Miriam had insisted that they probably wouldn't be able to eat for a week, Edie Bergson had pressed a parcel on her as "a little something you'll want before you go to bed." And the next morning as the rabbi recited his morning prayers, she took a brisk walk to the neighborhood grocer to get the few things they would need for breakfast. Dinner, the Sabbath meal, they were going to have at the Bergsons'.

It was while they were having their second cup of coffee that the doorbell rang, and there was Chief Lanigan when she opened the door.

"How did you know we were back?" asked the rabbi.

"David, David, how many times do I have to explain to you that I have to know what's going on in the town. I assumed you were coming back when the men in the cruiser reported your sidewalk and steps had been shoveled. I knew Miriam wouldn't be able to prepare Thanksgiving dinner with all the stores closed, and you certainly were not going to go to a restaurant. So that meant that you'd been invited by someone, and they'd arranged to have your place shoveled so you'd be able to get back here without having to plow through snow."

The rabbi nodded. "That's right. We had dinner at the Bergsons'. He's president of the temple, you know."

"I know. And your successor, Rabbi Selig, was there, too."

"And how do you know that?"

"His car was parked outside the Bergson house." He sipped at the coffee Miriam had automatically set before him, and said, "You know a Professor Kent at your school, David?"

"I've met him." Then, "Tell me, Hugh, did you just drop by to say hello or are you into something?"

Lanigan chuckled. "Mostly to say hello, but there was a little incident that kind of interested me. I tried to keep it quiet and I had it reported on the blotter as a case of trespass, but actually Mrs. Selig reported that she'd spotted a Peeping Tom peering in at her bedroom window."

The rabbi nodded slowly. "Yes, Al Bergson told me about it."

"Did he tell you that Rabbi Selig went to see Miller the next day and told him if he saw this Professor Kent on his property again, he'd punch him in the nose or throw him over the hedge?"

The rabbi shook his head.

"Well, he did."

"I'm sure he was just joking. Did Professor Miller take it seriously?"

"I don't think so, but his mother evidently did. It seems a

strange thing for a rabbi to say even as a joke. Would you ever have said something like that, David? I mean when you were a young man? When you first came here?"

"No-o, I don't think so."

"I don't think you would have," said Lanigan. "And I don't think Father Joe Tierny, our pastor, would either. But his curate, Father Bill, might. And do you know why? Because he works out at the gym. He works out with those machines and lifts weights just as your Rabbi Selig jogs. You get caught up in physical culture, and you're apt to think of physical solutions to problems."

"Perhaps you're right," said the rabbi with a smile.

Sunday saw a marked rise in temperature and the snow began to melt a little. Sergeant Aherne was behind the wheel of the cruiser, with Officer Ben Otis, who was nearing retirement, on the passenger seat beside him. As they came to the sign at the foot of Rabbi Selig's driveway that marked the town's limits, Otis said, "Pull over to the sidewalk, will you?"

"What for?"

"I've got to take a leak."

"Jeez, this is the third time we've stopped. You have to go a lot."

"It's these pills the doctor gave me, supposed to be good for my blood pressure."

Aherne brought the car to a halt and Otis jumped out and hurried behind the signboard. A moment later, he called out, "Hey, Tim, c'mere a minute."

"What's up?"

"Look." Otis pointed to a patent leather shoe and a stockinged foot rising from it.

Aherne knelt and with gloved hands began pulling at the

snow. The outline of a body was clearly visible, albeit covered with snow. He uncovered the head. "Jeez, that's the guy who was peeping in the window in the house up there."

"He must have slipped and fallen, struck his head, and then been buried by the falling snow."

"Yeah, could be. Look, you wait here and I'll call in to the station house."

Chapter 26

Y OU'RE sure it's the same man you saw on the porch on the house up there?" asked Lanigan.

"Oh, that's the fellow, all right," said Aherne.

"And you brought him to the Miller house on Evans Road?"

"That's right."

"All right. Go on up there and bring Miller down here." Then turning to the photographer, he said, "Take some pictures away from the body."

"Away from the body?"

"Yeah. Stand right under the ledge and focus on the triangle. I want to show that the snow there is smooth, fallen snow. The snow under the ledge is plowed snow. I want you to show that."

"Got it."

Lanigan stood beside him, suggesting various shots he wanted him to take.

From the road came a blast from an automobile horn. Lanigan called to the cruiser, "You got Miller with you? Bring him up here."

To Miller, wearing a stocking hat, a heavy muffler around his neck, his feet encased in overshoes, he said, "You know this man?"

"It's Professor Kent, Malcolm Kent, Clark Professor of Literature at Windermere."

"You don't seem surprised to see him here like this."

"The officer told me why you wanted me."

"You shouldn't have done that, Sergeant," said Lanigan.

"Don't blame him," said Miller. "I'm running a temperature and I assure you I wouldn't have come if he hadn't told me why you wanted me."

"All right. You can take him back now. I'll drop by and see you at your house," he said to Miller.

Later, after he'd had Lieutenant Jennings come to take charge, he proceeded to the Miller House. It was Mrs. Miller who opened the door in answer to his ring. As she led him to the living room where her son was, she admonished, "Now, don't you go badgering him. He's sick, poor boy."

"Aw, Ma!"

"Well, I'm going to sit right here and listen."

Lanigan smiled. "That's fine, Mrs. Miller. I just want to get this business cleared up as soon as possible." He turned to Miller. "Now, were you expecting this Professor Kent Wednesday? Was he coming to visit you?"

"Well, he was and he wasn't. You see, he was going to a formal wedding reception up in Breverton, at the country club there. So he thought he'd come here and spend the early evening with us, perhaps have a bite to eat, and then I was to drive him up there. Then when it was over, he was going to phone me, and I'd go up and get him and bring him down here for Thanksgiving. Unless, of course, someone at the reception invited him to stay over."

"Seems like you were going to a lot of trouble for him," remarked Lanigan.

"Well, he'd gone to a lot of trouble for me," said Miller.

"That's so?"

"Damn right. See, I'm not much of a scholar; I've never pub-lished and I didn't know how long I'd be allowed to stay at Win-dermere. So I sort of lined up another job—in Arizona because I thought it would be good for my mother's asthma."

"He's always thinking of me," remarked Mrs. Miller.

"It was a two-year junior college, and a technical school at that. When I told him about it, he practically ordered me to turn it down. When I pointed out that I didn't have tenure here and could be dropped anytime, he said he'd get it for me. And he did."

"Yes, I can see why you'd be grateful. And you, ma'am, are you glad your son didn't take the Arizona job?"

"Well, I have a sister there who is also troubled with asthma, and she says the climate is good for her; it's so dry. Matter of fact, I'm going out to visit her tomorrow if Thor is better. But I wouldn't stand in Thorvald's way for anything. My Thorvald is a professor in an eastern college, right in Boston, at that; well . . . and being a friend of Professor Kent, whose folks started the col-lege, and knowing all those important people . . ." Her voice trailed off as she considered the possibilities for the future.

"But I didn't drive in Wednesday," Miller went on. "I had trou-ble with my windshield wiper, so I parked at Swampscott station and took the train in. Professor Kent suggested we could take his car. That was all right with me, but I had an appointment and told him I'd drop by afterwards. Then he said that the radio re-ported that the roads were clear and he might drive up by him-self. I called his house when I was through, but he wasn't there and I figured he'd gone ahead. I wasn't worried because he's a good driver. I called here to ask if he'd got in yet, and Ada Bron-son said he hadn't, so I figured he'd gone straight up to Brever-ton instead of stopping here. I took the five thirty-two and got to Swampscott just before six. I was a little concerned that maybe he might be sore at me, so I waited up till past midnight on the chance that he'd drive up after the reception. When he didn't, I assumed he'd been invited to stay over at someone's house for Thanksgiving dinner."

"And you weren't troubled that you didn't hear from him all weekend?"

"He wasn't one for telephoning. But no, I wasn't worried about his safety. The roads had been cleared, and he was a careful driver. I figure what happened was that when it got dark, he parked someplace and decided to take the bus. He got off at the sign where he usually got off when he came by bus. Then he went up the right-of-way, on the outside of the hedge because I had warned him against using the driveway, and he'd either stumbled, or maybe had a heart attack—that's a bit of a hill, and it was cold and snowing—and had tumbled off the ledge."

"I think," said Mrs. Miller very deliberately, "that he came up the driveway and that rabbi feller saw him and threw him over the hedge and he fell off the ledge."

"Oh, Ma, that was just a kind of joke."

"Well, that's what he said he was going to do."

"That's a terrible accusation, Mrs. Miller," said Lanigan severely, "and you'd better not repeat it. You might find yourself being sued for more money than your son is apt to make in a lifetime."

He had risen and was on the point of leaving when a thought occurred to him. "He was not wearing overshoes or even rubbers when he was found, just his patent leather pumps. Doesn't that seem strange to you?"

"No, not really," said Miller. "He was a bit of a dandy, Professor Kent was. There's a sort of covered walk from his back door to the shed where he kept his car. Then if he drove here, he'd park right in front of the house, and it is just a step or two to the door.

And if I drove him up to the country club, naturally I'd drive him to the foot of the stairs, which would certainly have been shoveled."

Lanigan nodded and made for the door.

Chapter 27

B Y the time Lanigan got back to the scene, the body had been removed and the area marked by yellow tape stretched on iron rods that had been pounded into the frozen ground. In addition to the policemen, there were a few people standing around, with those who had been there earlier describing to later arrivals where the body had been found, how he was dressed, and what he looked like. From his car, Lanigan spotted Rabbi Selig and hailed him and beckoned him over to the car. He opened the door on the passenger side and said, "Get in, Rabbi. Might as well be comfortable. Looks mighty cold out there."

"It is. Thanks."

"Did you get a look at the body, Rabbi?"

"No, he was covered and they were just taking him off when I got here."

"Well, he was the fellow that we picked up in response to a call from your wife."

"The Peeping Tom?"

"That's right."

Rabbi Selig shook his head slowly, incredulously.

"Who shoveled your driveway, Rabbi?" Lanigan asked.

"I did, but I didn't shovel. I have a snowblower."

"That's so? And when did you do it? What time?"

"I plowed twice; the first time just after my wife left for her class in Salem. That would be a little after two, I'd say. And I just plowed a strip in the driveway so she could get back. But then she called in the early evening and said she was having some people over, her class, because they were finishing a section and celebrating. So I plowed the whole terrace because she said there'd be half a dozen cars or more."

"And what time was that?"

"Let's see, the evening service starts at half past six, so I started around half past five and finished a little after six. Is it important?"

"Yes, it's important because it gives us the time. See, he was lying on plowed snow, not falling snow."

"You mean if I had looked over the ledge, I would have seen him?"

"Probably not, since the snow continued to fall for some time and it covered him. Do you go to the evening services every night?"

"No, not every night. Some nights I recite the prayers at home. If I'm tired, or not feeling well . . ."

"Then why did you feel you had to go Wednesday when the weather was so bad?"

"I had to go *because* the weather was so bad. You see, some people come because they are in mourning, or because it is the anniversary of the death of a member of the family. There's a special prayer they recite, but it can only be said in a public service, not if they're praying alone at home. Well, when the weather is bad, it's sometimes hard to get the ten men required for a minyan, a public service, so I make a point of attending if the weather is bad."

"And you need ten men?"

"Uh-huh. Like a quorum, or twelve men for a jury."

Lanigan nodded.

It was a troubled Rabbi Selig who made his way back to his house. "It was that Peeping Tom guy," he told his wife in answer to her question of what it was all about.

"Oh, no!"

"Yup. And he was lying on plowed snow, which means—"

"I know what it means. And you told that Miller person that you'd throw him over the hedge if he came on our property again. Dana, we're in trouble. We certainly don't need a scandal."

"So what do I do?"

"Maybe you ought to see a lawyer. How about talking to Lew Baumgold?"

"Why Lew Baumgold?"

"Because he's not a member of the congregation."

"Yeah."

❖   ❖   ❖

No sooner had Rabbi Selig left the car than Lieutenant Jennings sauntered over and took his place on the passenger seat of the car. He was a tall, gangling man of sixty, with a prominent Adam's apple that bobbed as he talked, and with teary blue eyes at which he kept dabbing with a handkerchief. "So what do we do now, Hugh?"

"We'll get the make and license number of his car and notify all garages and police stations here to Boston to be on the lookout for it."

"If he parked on the street, he was plowed in, and you'll get no results until we get a thaw. And if he parked in one of those big garages like the one they've got at the airport, that could take days, too. You give them the number and they say they'll look. But they're busy and they wait until one of the attendants is free, maybe on his lunch hour. And if a car drives in to park and the hood is still warm, he gets up on the hood to warm his arse while he eats his lunch. And if the guy left one of the doors unlocked, the son of a bitch gets into the car and has his lunch there."

"So what do you suggest?"

"Look, Hugh, the guy is from Boston, and he's wearing a tuxedo, so he may be somebody important or social, so Boston is going to take over sooner or later."

"So?"

"So Bradford Ames, the Suffolk County assistant D.A., is in town. Maybe he came to see if the storm caused any damage to his place on the Point, or maybe he had some people over for Thanksgiving. His car is still there, so why not let him carry the ball."

"Oh, I'll let him know. Or he might have heard of it already, and he'll call me."

Chapter 28

T H E call came a little after ten o'clock at night. Chief Lanigan, already in pajamas, robe, and slippers, was having a nightcap as he leafed through the sports section of the Sunday paper. In answer to his hello, a voice he knew well said, "It's Luigi, Hugh."

"Not Luigi Tomasello, the senior assistant district attorney."

"None other than the same, Hugh, if this is the chief of police of Barnard's Crossing."

"Where you calling from?"

"From the office."

"Don't you have Sundays off?"

"You don't have it off every week either, Hugh."

"No, but I usually work a forty-hour week. Don't they have that in Lynn yet?"

"Look, Hugh, let's cut the chitchat. I want to know if you have the pics on the Kent case processed yet."

"I suppose we have. I haven't spoken to the photographer since he took them this morning. Why?"

"Because Bradford Ames wants to see them. Can you get them to him first thing tomorrow morning?"

"What's he got to do with them? It's an Essex County case."

"Well, now it's a Suffolk County case."

"How come?"

"The preliminary autopsy showed no water in the lungs, and there would have been if he'd been alive when he fell or was dropped in the snow. There's also a contusion on the forehead—"

"That could have come from falling on a rock. There was one right under his head."

"Sure, Hugh, but there was also discoloration from blood coagulation on his buttocks and backs of his thighs. He was lying on his front, so the coagulation should have been in front. Those are just preliminary findings. It may turn out to be heart failure or stroke, and subsequent death from the cold. Bradford Ames thinks it might be a car-jack case. And you know my boss; any chance he sees of getting out of a tough job, he'll grab. Besides, this one could be bad politically."

"How do you mean politically?"

"Oh, you know. With that Peeping Tom business, he'd have to go after that new rabbi you have, and the Jews might resent that. And that could hurt him in the next election."

"Yeah, I get the picture."

"So if you'd arrange to get those pics to Ames first thing in the morning . . ."

"I'll bring them in myself, Luigi. Okay?"

On the chance that the Smalls had not yet returned to the city, Lanigan called. Miriam answered the phone. In response to his query, she said, "We're going in tomorrow morning. Al Bergson offered to take us to the train at Swampscott, but we didn't like to impose on him, so we're taking the bus."

"Don't bother, Miriam. I've got to go to Boston, so I'll drive you in."

It was before nine the next morning that he drove up to the Small house. He inched his way through the narrow opening in the mound of plowed snow and mounted the steps. To the rabbi, who opened the door in response to his ring, he said, "You hear what happened?"

"It was on the local news report on the radio."

Lanigan held up the folder he had taken with him. "Want to see the pictures?"

"Not particularly." ·

"Aw, c'mon. It will give us extra identification. You knew him."

"Just barely."

"But enough to recognize him." He opened the folder. "This is how he looked when we uncovered him. He was lying facedown. And this is how he looked when we turned him over. Pretty, isn't he? In his tuxedo showing under his fine overcoat, with patent leather pumps nice and shiny, like he's been prepared for his wake."

"No rubbers or overshoes?"

"Nope. Miller says he was a bit of a dandy and wouldn't be likely to wear them unless he positively had to. If he were going to stop off there, the steps and the bit of sidewalk in front of them would be clear, and the same if he were planning to go straight on to the country club in Breverton."

Miriam came in from the kitchen with two cups of coffee. "The last," she announced, "before I wash out the percolator." She set them down and then returned to the kitchen to wash the breakfast dishes.

Lanigan took a sip and said, "Boston is taking over, which is why I'm bringing the pictures in, but I still have an interest in what happened. Now, here's what I want you to do, David. I want you to ask around about Kent—"

"I'm not in the police business," said the rabbi.

"You've helped us before."

"Then it was a member of my congregation who was involved."

"Well, don't kid yourself, David. Your congregation, at least its rabbi, is involved in this. This guy was caught peeping in the window at the rabbi's wife undressing. And you remember he told Miller he'd throw him over the hedge if he caught him trespassing again."

"But none of that was reported in the newspaper."

"David, David, you think in a small town like Barnard's Crossing we get our news by reading the newspaper? Most of the local news we get through gossip. And you know what happens to a story when it's passed from one person to another."

The rabbi nodded gloomily. "All right. I'll keep my ears open."

Lanigan grunted in satisfaction. "I don't for a moment think Selig threw him off the ledge, or even saw him. Selig used a snowblower twice. The first time was around two o'clock, and the second time around half past five. I figure Kent came along around five, maybe had a heart attack and fell. By the time Selig starts plowing the second time, Kent is covered, at least to the extent where he wouldn't be seen by Selig. And then he gets covered real good by the snow from the second plowing. We know that because he was lying on plowed snow—as well as covered by it."

"That seems reasonable."

"It stopped snowing around half past six. Now, if we'd had any sort of thaw, maybe part of the body would have been exposed, but it was bloody cold the whole weekend, except we had bright sun Sunday morning when the patrolman peed and uncovered his shoe. And it looks as though this cold is apt to continue for a while, something about the jet stream coming down from Canada."

Miriam came into the room again, but this time she had her coat on and a scarf covering her head. "I'm ready," she said.

"Yeah," said Lanigan, rising. "Let's go."

Chapter 29

No sooner had Bradford Ames taken jurisdiction of the Kent case for Suffolk County than he immediately got in touch with Detective Sergeant Schroeder of Boston's homicide squad, whom he most liked to work with. Because he came from a wealthy family, Bradford Ames, a chubby, chuckly man of fifty-five whose expensive clothes never seemed to quite fit him, had been able to go into that branch of law he was most interested in since he was not concerned about making his living at it. He was primarily interested in criminal law and litigation, so through family influence he had joined the district attorney's office even before he passed the bar exam. And he had remained on year after year, his influence steadily growing. District attorneys came and went. They were political figures primarily, and if they were smart, and most of them were, they permitted themselves to be led by him and profited by his instruction and direction.

As for Sergeant Schroeder, a tall, thin, dour man with a black crew cut now graying at the temples, he was the same age as Ames, and although he did not understand the district attorney's sense of humor, or his enthusiasms, he was fully aware of the effect of his preference for him on his standing in the Boston Police Department.

"The Kent case, Sergeant," said Ames. "We'll be handling it. I've just spoken to Assistant District Attorney Tomasello of Essex, and he tells me we'll have the photos tomorrow morning. Chief Lanigan—remember him?—will probably bring them in himself. Now I'd like you to go over to the college and find out who saw Kent last."

❖   ❖   ❖

The English office was on the second floor of the Administration Building, and on Monday morning, when Sergeant Schroeder came a few minutes before ten o'clock, it was a busy place with the various members of the department hurrying in to gather books and notes and then hurrying out to meet their ten-o'clock classes. Since he was not in uniform, they assumed he was perhaps a book salesman who was there to see Professor Sugrue, the head of the department.

He reached into his pocket and brought out the leather folder in which his badge was pinned so that he could show it and stop one of them, but the hurried exodus continued, and within a couple of minutes only one was left, and he was striding toward the door.

"Hey, just a minute—" he called.

But the other said, "Sorry, mister, but I haven't got a minute. I've got a class at Wentworth, which is at the end of the street. Professor Sugrue will be along in a couple of minutes. He's probably the one you want to see." And he was through the door and gone.

Sergeant Schroeder was annoyed. He was not used to having his authority flouted, but short of chasing after the man, there was nothing he could do. So he wandered about the room, studying the bulletin board, looking curiously at whatever papers had been left exposed on desktops, and was in the middle of reading a handwritten letter, seemingly from a student explaining a fail-

172

ure to hand in a paper on time, when Professor Sugrue entered the room.

The sergeant looked up guiltily at the tall, gangling figure who was looking at him questioningly, and stammered, "I'm just waiting around to see a Professor Sugrue."

"I am Professor Sugrue."

"Oh, swell, I'm Sergeant Schroeder, Boston Police Department, Homicide." And this time he was able to show his badge.

"Homicide? This is in reference to Professor Kent? I thought he'd had a heart attack."

"Well, he may have. But there's some question about it, so we're investigating."

"So how can I help you?"

"For one thing, I'd like to know who saw him last before the Thanksgiving vacation."

"Let me see." Professor Sugrue flipped the cover on a small metal box and thumbed through the cards it contained. "Let me see, Wednesday. Professor Kent had a four-o'clock on Wednesday, and so did Professor Fine, Professor Handy, and Professor Morrow. Those are late-afternoon and evening classes, you understand, and I'm under the impression that all of them canceled their classes for the day because of the storm, you know. Called in before noon. Handy and Morrow come from a distance; one is from Gloucester and the other from Ipswich. Professor Fine lives in Newton, but he walks with a cane, and I supposed he thought the going would be treacherous."

"Yeah, I know. I know Professor Fine."

"Do you? Of course, Professor Kent was not affected since he lives next door, you might say. I suppose I should say 'lived' instead of 'lives.' "

"How about those with three-o'clock classes that end at four? They might have seen him."

"Three o'clock is the last hour of the regular session. Let's see,

Professor Miller has a three-o'clock, Mondays, Wednesdays, and Fridays. But he didn't come in today; he has a bad cold. Then there's Sarah McBride. She's really Mrs. Baumgold, Mrs. Lew Baumgold. Her husband is a lawyer in Salem, but she calls herself Ms. McBride, at least here. She should be along in a few minutes. She has an eleven-o'clock."

"And I don't suppose you saw him, did you? You weren't around that afternoon?"

"As it happens, I was, but I didn't see him. I was in the library most of the afternoon. I got back here to the office around a quarter past four. Miller and McBride must have gone by that time. Oh, someone came in to ask about Professor Kent. A Mr. er—some Italian-sounding name. He'd been once or twice before to see Professor Kent. He came in to ask if Professor Kent was teaching a class. He'd gone to his house and rung and knocked and received no answer, so he thought he might be teaching a class. I told him he wasn't, and he said he'd go back and try again, that maybe he'd been tied up, been in the john."

"How did you know he wasn't teaching his class?" asked the sergeant.

"Oh, on my way from the library, I passed his classroom. It was empty, and there was a notice on the door saying that Professor Kent would not be meeting his four-o'clock class." He pushed aside the card file and leaned back in his chair. "Is there anything else?"

"Yeah. Was he liked in the department? Did he have any enemies, you know, guys who didn't like him?"

"We-el, he didn't have many friends." Sugrue was obviously uncomfortable. "He was an old man and had been here longer than anyone else in the department, and some felt that he took advantage of his seniority to—to—"

"To throw his weight around?"

"I'm sure he didn't intend to. It was just that—that—er—that other people might have interests or attitudes that differed from his. Oh, here's Sarah McBride now. Maybe she saw him. I'll have to run along now. Appointment with the dean."

❖　❖　❖

"You are Mrs. Baumgold," said Sergeant Schroeder.

"Guilty," she replied. "But here I'm Sarah McBride."

"I am Sergeant Schroeder, Boston Homicide." He showed her his badge. "Wednesday, you had a class at three o'clock which ended at four."

"I had a class at three, but I ended at half past instead of four."

"Why?"

"Because of the storm, of course. Less than half the class came, and those who did welcomed an early start. And it was the start of the vacation."

"So you ended the class and came back here to the English office?"

"That's right."

"Was anyone here?"

"Yes, Professor Kent was sort of lounging around. He asked me to go to the room where he gives his four-o'clock and post a notice saying he would not be meeting his class."

"And you went?"

She nodded.

"Why didn't he do it himself?"

She shrugged, then said, "He liked to have people do things for him."

"And then you came back here?"

"Just to get my things."

"And he was still here?"

"That's right, although he kept saying he had to go home and get dressed for this party he was going to. But I just got my things and hurried out."

175

"Why?"

"Because if I were alone with him, he'd be apt to get avuncularly affectionate, put his arm around my shoulder to show me something interesting. That sort of thing."

"What class did you have before this one?"

"I had a one-o'clock."

"All present for that one?"

"No, only five out of thirty showed up. I cut that class short, too."

"So why didn't you cancel your three-o'clock? I gather from Professor Sugrue that most of the other members of the department canceled their classes for the day."

"Well, I sort of had to hang around. Lew, my husband, was in town. He had business in the courthouse. He lives in Barnard's Crossing and we were going to spend Thanksgiving there. The original plans were that he would pick me up here and we'd drive home when he got through. But he didn't call, so I figured he was tied up. He called me later in the afternoon to tell me that he hadn't driven in; he'd taken the bus. I didn't care to take the bus out to Barnard's Crossing and then wade through a foot or more of snow for a couple of blocks to get to the house. So we agreed I'd come out by train Thursday morning and he'd pick me up at Swampscott station. And that's what we did."

"Did your husband know about this—this avuncular affection of Kent's?"

"Oh, yes. And so did the members of the department."

"Didn't your husband mind?"

"Of course he did. He wanted to come and see him and read him the riot act, but I persuaded him not to."

"Why? Why didn't you want him to tell him off?"

"Because I'd lose my job."

"You mean he'd tell Professor Sugrue to fire you?"

"Oh, he wouldn't tell Sugrue. And I don't mean that I'd get a notice from Prex telling me to clean out my desk. I wouldn't be fired in the middle of the year. I just wouldn't be reappointed next year. You see, I don't have tenure, and I'm the only member of the department without a Ph.D. Professor Kent doesn't have one either, but that's different; he has tenure, for one thing, and he's got a kind of drag with the trustees, as near as I can make out."

"You mean he might tell the trustees not to renew your contract, and they'd do it?"

"Oh, I don't suppose he'd do it that way. He'd probably tell them that he'd been watching my work and thought they ought to hire someone with more experience. That sort of thing."

"And your husband? When you told him not to protest or anything, he just let it go?"

"He doesn't like it, of course. He told me to stay out of his way. And that's what I do. If he's alone in the office, I stay clear of it. Once or twice he called and asked me to get a book out of the library for him and bring it over to his house, but I always managed to get out of it."

"Your husband, he's with some law firm?"

"Uh-huh. Schofield, Petrillo and Langerham, in Salem."

Schroeder jotted the name down in his notebook.

Chapter 30

MOST of the class were already seated, and the rest came in along with the rabbi as he entered his office. No sooner was he seated in his leather chair than one of the students called out, "Hey, Rabbi, did you see this morning's paper? Did you see the story on Professor Kent?"

"Was he coming to see you?"

"Nah, he was going to see Professor Miller. That's what the *Herald* said."

"But the *Globe* said he was found near the rabbi's house."

"Not this rabbi. There's another rabbi in Barnard's Crossing."

The rabbi held up both hands in a call for silence. Then he said, "I'll tell you what I know, and then perhaps we can get on with the proper work of the class. The body of Professor Kent was found in a field adjoining the lawn of Rabbi Selig's house. Rabbi Selig succeeded me as rabbi of the Barnard's Crossing Temple. It is presumed that Professor Kent was on his way to visit Professor Miller, who lives just beyond Rabbi Selig. The cause of death has not been determined. He was well along in years, so a heart attack or a stroke is a possibility. The extreme cold probably had something to do with it, and the snow kept him from being seen and possibly rescued. Not too many were out on foot during the storm, but he might have been seen from a passing car, which I am sure would then have stopped to check. Now, if we can get to—"

"But, Rabbi—"

"Don't the police in Barnard's Crossing—"

It occurred to the rabbi that the informal setting of his office made teaching under the present circumstances all but impossible. When he tried, he caught whispers like, "Did you ever take a course with the guy?" and "Naw, he was supposed to be a hard marker."

Finally he dismissed them with, "I'm afraid your minds are not on our subject today, so I'll end the session now. For next time, please read the last chapter of Isaiah and think about its implications."

They filed out, still talking about Professor Kent, but Sarah McBride remained behind. He looked at her inquiringly.

She waited until the last student had filed out, and then said, "A policeman came to question me."

"Came to your house? When? This morning?"

"No, here. He was here when I arrived around half past ten. He'd been talking to Professor Sugrue. He wasn't in uniform. He was a detective, a sergeant. Sergeant Schroeder, he said his name was. He was trying to find the last person who had seen Kent alive. So then he started to ask about Lew. Did Lew know him? Did he know Lew was from Barnard's Crossing? Would Lew have offered to drive him there? When I said Lew didn't have his car with him, his face lit up, and that frightened me. Was I getting Lew in trouble? So I told him I had a class, and he said, 'Okay, I'll see you afterwards.' I didn't tell him it was a class I was taking, yours, and not one I was giving. I was afraid if I said it was one I was taking, he'd have me skip it and keep me there. You see, Sugrue had left and there were just the two of us."

"But you've seen Lew, haven't you, since last Wednesday, I mean?"

"Oh, yes, we spent the weekend together."

"Then why are you concerned?"

She shook her head. "I've never had dealings with the police, not even for a traffic violation. It was his attitude, I suppose, more than anything else."

"Hostile? Suspicious?"

"Both. I had the feeling that he wouldn't believe anything I might say; that he expected me to lie and that he would catch me out if I did."

The rabbi nodded, smiling. "Yes, that sounds like Sergeant Schroeder."

"Oh, you know him?"

"When I was last here, a few years ago, something came up, and I found myself involved with the good sergeant."

"I wouldn't mind so much if it were just me he was suspicious of, but I don't want to say anything that's apt to get Lew in trouble."

"Lew is a lawyer, I think you told me. I should think he'd be able to take care of his own interests."

"Yes, I guess so." She smiled. "When next I see Sergeant Schroeder, I'll tell him everything that happened."

"But nothing happened, did it?"

"No, but Sergeant Schroeder strikes me as the sort of man who can make something out of nothing."

Chapter 31

R A B B I Small left the school shortly after noon. As he walked along Clark Street a car drove up and came to a halt beside him. The front window on the passenger side was lowered and the chubby face of Bradford Ames, the senior assistant district attorney of Suffolk County, appeared, leaning out awkwardly from the driver's seat. "Rabbi Small," he called, and as the rabbi approached, "Lanigan said you were teaching here now, and I was going to look you up." He threw open the door, saying, "Hop in, hop in, Rabbi."

"Where are you going?"

"Just to the corner, to Kent's house. I want to have a look-see. You knew him, of course."

"Just by sight. I was sort of introduced to him. I said, 'How do you do,' but other than that, I've never spoken to him. I don't think he answered even when we were introduced."

"Self-important, was he? Or didn't he like rabbis, or the people they serve?"

"I don't know."

"Ah, here we are. Come on in, Rabbi." He mounted the two or three steps and knocked on the door while the rabbi peered curiously through the glass panel on the side. The door was opened by Sergeant Schroeder, who said, "Oh, hello. We're about finished."

"Good. Look who I brought you, Sergeant. You remember Rabbi Small, don't you?"

"Oh yeah. He involved in this?"

"Oh no. Rabbi Small teaches here. I just happened to catch him as I was driving by." He swiveled around to survey the hall and the room beyond. He pointed at a shallow basket beside the wall near the door. It contained a pair of rubbers and a pair of overshoes. "Did you get a picture of that, Sergeant? It's most important."

"Why?" asked the sergeant.

"Because according to the pictures Chief Lanigan brought in this morning—brought them in himself—a good man, Lanigan. Remember him?"

The sergeant nodded. "Uh-huh."

"Well, according to the pictures, he wasn't wearing any rubbers. Under his melton coat he was wearing a tuxedo and patent leather pumps. Lanigan thought they might have slipped off as he plodded through the snow, but now we know he wasn't wearing rubbers because they're right there."

"Maybe he had another pair in the car," Schroeder suggested.

"True, and we haven't found the car yet. And if he parked on the street somewhere, and was plowed in, we might not find it until we get a thaw. Coming here, I passed streets where there were rows of cars, bumper to bumper, and all almost buried in the snow."

"Lanigan spoke to a Professor Miller, who thought he was coming to his house. Miller thought he might have parked somewhere along the road because he found the driving too difficult and taken the bus; that he got off at the bus stop at this rabbi fellow's driveway. There's a hedge there, and the other side of it is a right-of-way to this Miller's house. What do you think, Rabbi?"

"I didn't know Professor Kent well. I know only that as far as I'm concerned, it would have to be a matter of life or death before I would have got behind the wheel of a car during that storm Wednesday afternoon. But then, I'm a very nervous driver."

"Well, I drove out to Barnard's Crossing myself in the early part of the afternoon," said Ames. "It was pretty bad then, but the State Road had been cleared. What are you suggesting?"

"We have a lot of people, students and faculty, living on the North Shore: Lynn, Salem, Beverly, Barnard's Crossing. Maybe he got one of them to drive him."

"Who?"

The rabbi shook his head. "I'm new here. I know where a few of my colleagues live, but that's about it."

"All right. You might ask around, Sergeant. Maybe there are one or two that he used regularly."

"Will do. How about the desk over there?" he asked, nodding at the open door of the study leading off the hall where they were standing. "You want me to go over the papers in the desk?"

"No, I'll have one of the assistant D.A.s, someone with accounting experience." Idly curious, he pulled open the wide center drawer. In the pencil ledge there were pencils and ballpoint pens, to be sure, but there was also a single key. "That looks like a safe-deposit key. And there's a number on it. In all likelihood, it will be in the same bank where he has a checking account. So you check with them, and I'll get a court order to open it. If he made a will, that's where he'd keep it."

"He banks with the Boston Trust. At least that's where he had a checking account. I bank there myself, the main bank on Washington Street. Chances are he uses the local branch because it's just around the corner from here. I know the manager, Mike

Sturgis, because he used to be at the main bank. I helped him once; a little trouble with his son. I'll bet he'd let us take a look at his safe-deposit box, if that's where it is, even without a court order, where it's a police matter, I mean."

Ames gave a gurgly chuckle. "There's no harm in trying. It could save us a little time. It's box 552."

❖ ❖ ❖

Michael Sturgis, short, fat, and with a wide, balding dome glistening with the perspiration of anxiety, drew out the box and said, "I'll have to be with you and watch."

"No problem," said Schroeder.

Sturgis took the box to one of the cubicles adjacent to the safe-deposit room. "Oh dear," he said, "three of us won't fit in here. Look, let's go to my office."

He set the box down on his desk and sat down in his swivel chair as Ames and Schroeder pulled over visitors' chairs. "All right, gentlemen, go ahead."

Ames opened the box and Schroeder took out his notebook. "Let's see, here's a little cardboard box, and it contains some jewelry. Here's a gold ring with three red stones. Rubies?"

"Probably garnets," said Schroeder.

Ames looked to Sturgis, who shook his head. "All right, just put down three red stones. I doubt if they're worth very much even if they're rubies. And here's a ring with an opal, and another with a green stone which could be an emerald, but could be just green glass. I suspect the latter since the ring is only silver. And here's a gold tooth and a gold fountain pen point. I think that's about all the jewelry. Now, here's an insurance policy, fifty thousand dollars, and the beneficiary is Lorraine Donofrio. Didn't you say, Sergeant, that Professor Sugrue said an Italian type came to the English office and asked for Kent?"

"Yeah, but it was a man, and Lorraine is a woman's name."

"True, but it could be her father or her husband. Ah, here's a will. Made out by Alan Spector of the firm of Spector and Dole. They'll probably come to see you in a day or two, Mr. Sturgis, as soon as they get letters testamentary. You don't have to tell them that we looked at this stuff."

He flipped the pages of the will. "Let's see, 'all books and other scholarly materials go to Windermere College.' What are other scholarly materials? Pencils? Pens? Eyeglasses? And the sole residual legatee is Josephine Lorraine Donofrio. You suppose it's the same one who is the beneficiary of the insurance policy? And that she doesn't always use her first name for some reason or other?"

"It could be a daughter," said Sturgis. "Lately, women have begun copying men. I've got a couple depositors whose names are the same as their mothers', like Jane Doe, Junior."

"Could be," said Ames. "We'll be finding out pretty soon. Ah, here's a promissory note for a thousand dollars and it's marked 'Paid.' It was signed by Lorraine Bixby and Antonio Donofrio. And it was made out to the Bixby Hair Salon, nineteen Blossom Street, Lynn. I'd say that clears things up a bit. Lorraine Bixby married Antonio Donofrio and then she gave birth to Josephine."

"What's that at the bottom in the manila envelope?" asked Schroeder.

"Looks like the manuscript for a book," said Ames. "Our Professor Kent was probably a secret author. No, it's a doctoral dissertation by an Oscar Horton, which was submitted to the University of Nevada in 1953. And the subject is 'Simeon Suggs, Twentieth-Century Poetaster.' Never heard of him."

"Why would old Kent keep it in his safe-deposit box?" asked Schroeder.

Ames shrugged. "Maybe he thought he ought to keep it. Do you have a safe-deposit box, Sergeant? No? Well, I have, and on the rare occasions when I go to it, I always wonder at the junk I have in it. I always think perhaps I ought to remove some of the papers I've stored, like my law diploma. I suppose if I had gone into general practice like most of my classmates, I might have had it framed to hang on my office wall. But I went into the D.A.'s office immediately after passing the bar. Actually, even before. And there's the notice that I'd passed the bar, and a clipping from the morning newspaper that gave the list of those who passed. Then there's my father's watch, a repeater."

"What's a repeater?"

"Oh, you don't know what that is? Well, it enabled you to tell the time in the dark. You pressed a button and a little bell rang the hours, and then the minutes in five-minute intervals. I am told it's quite valuable, so I suppose it would be a temptation to one of the succession of cleaning women I've had over the years. I suppose that's why I keep it in the safe-deposit box, along with my father's stickpins. My friend Charlie Waterhouse keeps his overshoes in his safe-deposit box."

"That so?" Sergeant Schroeder was used to Ames's prolixity and listened with only half an ear. "So I'll go to see this Donofrio," he said when Ames paused.

"No," said Ames decisively. "I'll ask Hugh Lanigan to see them."

"Why Lanigan?"

"Because they're in Lynn, which is Essex County, so it's really their baby." His real reason was that Schroeder, being from a large city and hence used to dealing largely with professional criminals, was apt to be somewhat peremptory in his attitude toward small-town citizens, who were inclined to view the police as friends and neighbors. "Besides," he went on, "I'd like you to concentrate on the college here. Talk to the people in the English Department. One of them might know something about Kent. Has there been anything more on the autopsy?"

"Nah, just what we got on the preliminary report—cardiac arrest. My guess is that's all we're going to get. And I suspect that's all there is. He was a little shrimp of a guy and he was over seventy. And he goes plowing through the snow during a blizzard, without no rubbers yet. So he gets a heart attack and falls down and the snow covers him."

Ames nodded. "I'm inclined to agree with you, but we've got to make sure, don't we?"

"Why? What's so important that we got to be sure?"

"Because lots of folks in Barnard's Crossing think maybe the rabbi of the Jewish temple there—what's his name? Selig, Rabbi Selig—think he may have knocked him over with his snowblower."

Chapter 32

T H E story had grown from telling to telling; Ada Bronson told her husband, who passed it on to the boys who came in for a beer at the Ship's Cabin. Mrs. Miller told it to a woman she met at the supermarket. Members of the police force may have mentioned it to their wives.

The story grew in all dimensions. The voyeurism became an attempt at entry, which became a forced entry and attempted rape, which became a physical attack ending in actual rape. The finding of the body underneath the ledge was explained by Selig's having caught sight of Kent and chased him, and he had slipped and fallen off. And this gave way to the story that Selig had seen him coming up the right-of-way and had directed the stream from his snowblower at him and knocked him off the ledge that way. And ultimately, that Selig had caught him and picked him up bodily and thrown him off the ledge.

The phone calls began coming in Tuesday morning, shortly after Rabbi Selig had returned from *shachriss*, the morning service. After a while, he stopped answering the phone, knowing that he would not miss anything important since the calls would register on the answering machine. Later in the afternoon, when he had a chance to play the messages back, he decided that he ought to consult with the president, Al Bergson.

First, however, he discussed it with his wife, who said, "You could be in trouble, Dana."

"You mean the temple might ask me to resign?"

"No, I mean you could be in trouble with the law. You threatened to pick him up and throw him over the hedge, and that's where he was found, over the hedge on the flat."

"Aw, c'mon. I'm pretty husky and he was a little shrimp of a guy, but no one would believe that I could pick up someone weighing at least a hundred and twenty or twenty-five pounds, and heave him over a four-foot hedge for a distance of about fifteen feet."

"Well, they could claim that he was on the other side of the hedge and you blew him over with a blast of snow from the snowblower. I think maybe you ought to see a lawyer."

"Yeah, and as soon as word got out that I had consulted a lawyer, people would take that as proof that I thought I might be guilty. Even though it was dark when I started to plow, I'm sure I would have seen him if he were coming up the path on the other side of the hedge."

"How about all those phone calls you got?"

"Well, practically every one of them favored me, thought I did the right thing."

"Which means they thought you did it."

"Ye-ah," he said reluctantly. "So what do I do?"

"Look, Dana, maybe it would be a good idea to talk to Rabbi Small."

"Why would I want to talk to David Small? What's he got to do with it? He has no position here now."

"He's lived here for twenty-five years, so he knows the town. Besides, he's supposed to be friendly with the police chief, this whatshisname, Lanigan. He could ask him what gives."

"I'll think about it."

As expected, Al Bergson was at the evening minyan. As soon as the service ended, Rabbi Selig approached him. "Got a couple of minutes, Mr. Bergson?"

"Sure, what can I do for you?"

Rabbi Selig waited until the rest had departed and he was alone with Bergson. Then he said, "I got a number of phone calls about this business last Sunday."

"As a matter of fact, so have I," said Bergson.

"That so?"

"Uh-huh, and so have some other members of the congregation."

"What do you think I ought to do?"

Bergson shrugged. Then, "Have the police spoken to you yet? Have you been questioned at all?"

"Well, yeah. See, that Sunday, when I saw the crowd at the foot of my driveway, I went down to see what it was all about. The police chief was in his car and he invited me over. So we sat in his car and talked for a while. He asked me when I'd plowed the driveway, and I told him. And that was all."

"Well, that might be the end of it, but I doubt it. You know, if Rabbi Small were in town, I'd go and see him, if I were you. He and Lanigan, the police chief, are thick as thieves. The Lanigans have eaten at the Small house on occasion, and David and Miriam have had tea at the Lanigans'. What's more, David Small has been helpful to Lanigan on more than one occasion."

"I could go into Boston and see him, couldn't I?"

"Sure you could, and I think you should. Here, I'll give you the phone number of the apartment where he's staying." He took a pencil and notebook from an inner pocket and wrote down the phone number. "Call him in the evening and make an appointment to see him either at his office in the college or at home."

"Thanks. And by the way, I don't think I'll come to the Board meeting this Sunday."

"No? Any particular reason?"

"Well, you got phone calls and you said some of the other members did, too. So I figure you'll be wanting to talk about it, and you'll be able to talk more freely if I'm not there."

Bergson nodded. "Okay."

"You drove in?" asked Rabbi Small, as he motioned his visitor to a chair and closed the door of his office so that they would not be disturbed. "Where did you park?"

"No, I came in by bus," said Rabbi Selig. "One of the reasons for my taking the house was that the bus stopped right at our driveway and if I had occasion to go into Boston, I wouldn't have to worry about finding a place to park."

"Good thinking," said Rabbi Small. "When I first came here, the dean said he'd try to arrange for my own parking space. He was unable to, though. Since moving to Brookline, I come in by streetcar. Very convenient."

"In the light of what happened, I'm not so sure that having the bus stop at my driveway is such an advantage. You know what happened?"

Rabbi Small nodded. "Chief Lanigan had business in Boston Monday and was kind enough to drive us in. He told me all about it on the way. It was not that he was making conversation; he felt that I was concerned because of the effect it might have on the congregation and on you."

"He thought I was involved?"

"He also wanted me to find out what I could about Professor Kent since I was in a position to inquire and he wasn't."

"But what did he think about me?" demanded Selig.

"As matters stand now, there are several possibilities that have to be considered; one, that he slipped off, perhaps as a result of a sudden heart attack; two, that you forced him off with a blast from your snowblower, either accidentally because you didn't see him, or intentionally because you wanted to pay him off for the, er—affront to your wife; and three, that you picked him up bodily and threw him off."

"But that's ridiculous—"

"Number three certainly; you'd have to be a giant to do it. But the possibility that you aimed your snowblower at him has to be seriously considered."

"And how are they going to prove that?"

"Unfortunately, they don't have to prove it. They would, to send you to jail, but they don't have to prove it to wreck your career and to inflict damage on the congregation. There are three elements that they look for: weapon—in this case, the snowblower; opportunity—he was coming along while you were plowing the snow; and motive. And you gave them that when you spoke to the Millers."

"So I'm sunk; my career is wrecked even if I don't go to jail."

"Oh no. Those are the possibilities that appear at the moment. The police have only just begun investigating the case. There is the possibility that he was actually killed elsewhere and then brought to Barnard's Crossing where his body was dumped. There is pretty good evidence that that's what happened, which is why Suffolk County has taken over the case."

"So what do I do now?"

"Nothing. Do nothing."

"Should I talk to a lawyer?"

"Only your wife. She's a lawyer, isn't she? I wouldn't engage a lawyer unless you are charged."

Chapter 33

WHEN Lanigan called his friend Bill Mulcahey, chief of police of the city of Lynn, he was surprised at the chortle his request elicited. "They sent you an invitation, too? Those dagos! I'll bet they sent one to the governor, too."

"What in hell are you talking about, Bill?"

"You asked if I had anything on Donofrio. Well, Vittorio Donofrio is retiring after forty years of service in the Highway Department. He got to be a foreman or something. And so the Italianos are giving him a banquet, on which, believe me, they won't lose any money."

"Vittorio Donofrio? No, this is Antonio Donofrio."

"Oh, Antonio, that's his son. He's a barber or hairdresser. Got a place near the railroad station. Let's see, it's—it's Bixby Hair Salon. He owns it, or he's married to the lady who owns it. What do you want him for?"

"I just want to talk to him."

❖   ❖   ❖

Inasmuch as the city of Lynn was only about ten or fifteen minutes' drive from the town of Barnard's Crossing, the townspeople were apt to do as much of their shopping in Lynn as they were apt to do locally. And they knew the city almost as well. Chief Lanigan knew where Bixby's Hair Salon was; he had a faint recollection of Amy having gone there once or twice in the past when her regular hairdresser had gone on vacation and her shop had been closed.

Having found out that Donofrio worked there, Lanigan, even though not in uniform, had no hesitation in driving up to the front of the shop and parking in front of the No Parking sign. He entered, and in response to the questioning look of Mrs. Bixby at the little manicurist table, he said, "I am Hugh Lanigan of the Barnard's Crossing Police Department," and he showed her his badge, which he drew from his jacket pocket.

"Yeah, I think I seen your picture in the *Examiner* a coupla times. You're the chief, aren't you? What can I do for you, Chief?"

"I wanted to talk to Antonio Donofrio."

"That's him." She nodded. "He'll be another ten, fifteen minutes, I'd say. Look, Chief, why'nt you sit down and let me do your nails."

"You figure he'll be free in ten or fifteen minutes? I'll come back—"

"I don't mean a regular manicure. I'll just clip them a little. No charge. It's just it'll look better than if you stand there leaning over and talking to me. From the outside, I mean; someone passing by who might know you. It's all right, you know. I have plenty men customers."

"All right." Lanigan sat down and extended a hand to the woman. They had been talking in low tones, a little above a whisper. Now she said in normal tones, "Why'nt you take your hat and coat off. You can hang them there on the rack."

"All right," he said good-naturedly, and got up and hung up his coat and deposited his hat on the shelf above it. When he sat down again, she said, "I'll bet it's about Professor Kent, isn't it?"

"What makes you think so?"

"Well, you're from Barnard's Crossing and his body was found in Barnard's Crossing, and they're not sure how he died. Mrs. Thorpe was saying—you know her? She's from Barnard's Crossing, or maybe Swampscott—well, she was saying that it was this young minister, or priest, or something—no, it wouldn't be a priest, not a Roman Catholic one—who knocked him off the ledge on account he caught him peeping in the window while his wife was undressing. It could be a Greek priest; they're allowed to marry. Well, it wouldn't surprise me, him peeping, I mean. He was always, you know, interested in the ladies. I mean he was always looking and you know—"

"You mean he was horny?"

She giggled. "I wouldn't have said it, but he was, sort of, especially when he got older."

"Oh, you knew him."

"Yes, I knew him, all right."

"He used to come here for a manicure?"

"Not here, but when I was a manicurist in this barbershop in Boston where he used to go for a haircut. That was a good twenty years ago. We got real friendly, and he told me he loved me. He wanted to marry me. He couldn't, of course, on account he was already married—to this sick old woman. He said she was going to die soon, and he wanted me to wait until then. But a girl has to think of her future, and as time goes on, she doesn't get younger. So when Tony asked me to marry him, I said yes."

"And how did Kent take it?"

"I guess he understood. He even lent us the money to buy this place. And from time to time, he's lent us money when we needed it. I guess he felt we were the only family he had. When my Josephine was born, he took out an insurance policy naming me as the beneficiary. She calls him Uncle Malcolm."

"And Tony?"

"He thinks he's like some kind of cousin of mine. And that's what I want him to think," she added severely.

"I'm not likely to tell him different," said Lanigan, "but I've got to talk to him."

"Oh, Tony is almost through with Mrs. Wilson and he'll be free for an hour. Look, why don't you go down to the café a couple of stores down the block, and I'll send Tony to meet you there when he gets through."

❖   ❖   ❖

"I went to see him, but I didn't get to see him," announced Donofrio as he made for Lanigan's table.

"Why don't you get yourself a cup of coffee," suggested Lanigan, "and we can talk about it."

"All right." He went to the counter, was given a mug of coffee, and returned to join Lanigan at the table. "The missus said you wanted to talk to me because I went to see Kent the day before Thanksgiving. So I did, but I didn't see him."

"What did you go for?"

"For money, what else?"

"He owed you?"

"Nah." Donofrio squirmed in his seat as he tried to explain. "It's like this: He's an old geezer, and Lorraine, and I guess me and Josephine, are the only family he's got. So here he is living in this big house, a regular mansion, in the Back Bay in Boston. And here are we, just barely managing. So what's he going to do with all his money? Give it to the college? He's got nobody else.

196

"So you know how it is when you're running a business. Something comes up; something doesn't go right."

"And if things didn't go right, you'd come to see him and he'd give you money? What kind of money?"

"Oh, a couple of hundred. Once he gave us a thousand."

"Us?"

"Yeah, the missus and me. For the shop."

"Oh, I see. You'd have—"

"Like a plumber's bill, or once it was the oil."

"You'd be short and you'd go to see him, and he'd help you out."

"That's right. Mostly for the shop, but once it was for the dentist for the missus."

"And why did you go to see him last Wednesday?"

"You seen the shop. Look at this street. What kind of trade can we draw? All we get is a bunch of old ladies, and that's because they've been with us for years. So I wanted to talk to him about modernizing the place; maybe do some advertising."

"I see, and what time did you get there last Wednesday?"

"Let's see, I took the three-forty from Lynn, which gets into North station at four-o-two. Then the streetcar to Kenmore. Must've been around a little after four. I rang the bell and I knocked. I waited around about five minutes, thinking he might be in the john or something. Then I went to his office in the school, thinking he might still be there. A guy there said he was going to some fancy party up at Breverton, and maybe he started out already. So I went back to the house and rang again. Again no answer. So I figured he'd gone off and I went away."

"And you came back here to Lynn?"

"Well, I had to grab a bite of supper, so I went to the North End where I got a lot of friends, and just hung around for a while."

"So you got home when?"

"Pretty late, I guess. Maybe around eleven. Look, Chief, I got to get back. I got somebody coming in a couple of minutes."

"All right." And Lanigan nodded in dismissal.

Chapter 34

AL Bergson rapped on the table with his knuckles and said, "All right, let's come to order."

"Shouldn't we wait for the rabbi?" asked Norman Salzman. "He was at the minyan, so he should be along pretty soon."

"No, he won't be coming today," said Bergson. "He thought we might be talking about him and the business of the body in the snow, and he didn't want to hamper our discussion."

"That's one sweet guy," said Irving Cohen.

"Maybe he didn't want us to—to maybe ask him questions about it," suggested Dave Block, who was inclined to be cynical.

"The secretary will read the minutes," Bergson announced, to stop further discussion.

The secretary read the minutes: "The meeting was called to order at nine-o-five—"

"Discussion."

"What's to discuss? Nothing happened."

"Oh yeah? How about the roof? Wasn't the Building Committee supposed to get bids to repair the roof?"

"So that comes in Committee Reports."

"Seems to me there was a long discussion about this Purim party the Sisterhood is planning."

"Yeah, but nothing was decided."

"But the secretary ought to mention there was a discussion."

"That was the week before," said the secretary, "and it was in the minutes of last week's meeting."

"Oh, I was absent last week. I had to go to New York, and I—"

"Hey, let's get on with the meeting. You can tell us about your adventures in the Big Apple after the meeting."

It was after ten o'clock when they got through with Old Business. Not that there was any old business to discuss, but as always, they found it pleasant to just sit around and talk. But finally Bergson was able to bring up the matter that concerned him. "Rabbi Selig came to see me about a bunch of phone calls he'd received."

"Yeah, I got some, too," said Larry Sobel, who was in the real estate business. "These guys were Gentiles. There were two of them, guys I showed some properties to. One said I should be proud of my rabbi, and the other said he didn't blame him."

"And what did you say?" asked Bergson.

"Well, I thanked them, but then I said I didn't know what they were talking about. One of them just laughed and hung up, but the other said that he could understand the rabbi pushing the guy over the ledge because he'd made a pass at the rabbi's wife."

Bergson nodded. "Anybody else get any calls?"

Three raised their hands. One said, "I got a call from a woman who said we ought to be ashamed to have a minister who was a murderer."

"Anybody else get any hostile calls?" asked Bergson.

"A guy called me, wouldn't give his name, but said he could understand how the rabbi felt, but that as a man of God, he didn't think he ought to resort to violence."

"And what did you say?"

"Pretty much what Larry said, that I didn't know what he was talking about. And he said, 'Aw, c'mon,' and hung up."

"Anybody else?" asked Bergson.

Andy Taitelbaum raised a timid hand. "I got a call from a fellow I went to school with. I bump into him every now and then, but he's never called me before. We talked for a couple minutes. You know, just kidded around, and then he says, 'I saw your rabbi jogging the other day. He's pretty good.' "

"And?"

"That's all. He says, 'Gimme a ring sometime, Andy.' And he hangs up."

"So he didn't say anything."

"I figure he thought maybe *I* would."

"Maybe he was ribbing you about your rabbi running around in shorts or a sweat suit."

"What's wrong with the rabbi jogging in a sweat suit?"

"Would you go to a doctor or even a lawyer if he wore Levi's; in his office, I mean?"

"Yeah, but Rabbi Selig doesn't wear a sweat suit when he comes to the temple."

Bergson rapped on the table. "All right, all right, let's get back to what this meeting is supposed to be about. This business may fade away and die out, or it may get worse and more of you might get phone calls. So let me set the record straight and tell you what happened as near as we can make out. First of all, keep in mind that Rabbi Selig had nothing to do with the guy's death, neither deliberate, nor by accident. So anybody who calls to tell you they admire the rabbi for what he did, you tell them flat out that he did nothing.

"This guy seems to have started out from Boston to go to a formal wedding reception in Breverton. Then, either his car broke down, or he parked it because the snow was getting heavier and he took the bus. Instead of taking the Breverton bus, which goes up the State Road, he took the Barnard's Crossing bus, which goes up the old Boston Road. And he got off at the rabbi's driveway because he had a friend living on Evans Road where he used to visit during the summer. He'd use the right-of-way alongside the rabbi's house to get to his friend's house. He was an old man and probably had a heart attack going up the hill on a cold, snowy day, and he fell off.

"Now, the rabbi plowed his driveway around two o'clock because the rebbetzin had to go to Salem where she was taking a course. Chances are the guy got off the bus around five, maybe a little after. And if he had a heart attack and fell, he got covered by the falling snow in a matter of fifteen minutes or a half hour at the most."

"Yeah, but the rabbi plowed again, didn't he?"

"That's right. The rebbetzin called to tell him she was bringing some people home for coffee and doughnuts around half past seven or eight. Since there would probably be several cars, the rabbi plowed the terrace at the head of his driveway, and went over the driveway again. And some of that plowed snow fell on this guy Kent, who was already covered. So if anyone calls to tell you what a great guy the rabbi is for hitting back because his wife was insulted, you tell him the rabbi did no such thing. Get it? Because in the long run it could hurt us with the community."

"Still, you got to admit that if we had a rabbi like Rabbi Small, a scholarly type, we wouldn't get any of this flak," said Jerry Andleman.

"Oh no? Well, for your information," said Taitelbaum, "my father told me that the first year Small was here, a girl's body was found in the bushes beyond the parking lot, and for a while it was thought that Small had something to do with it."

Chapter 35

CHIEF Lanigan sat at his desk in the station house and doodled on a pad as he thought about Professor Miller and his mother. Although he had recorded in his journal the occasion of his visits to the Miller house, he had made no notes on what had taken place while he was there. Thinking about it now, it seemed to him that Mrs. Miller was more supportive of Kent than her son had been. He wondered idly if it was because she was more emotional. Or was she perhaps personally involved with the man? He could not very well ask her, but it occurred to him that he might ask Ada Bronson since she "helped out" at the Millers' frequently.

He called out to the desk sergeant to have Sergeant Dunstable come in. Dunstable thought of himself as Detective Sergeant Dunstable because he did not wear a uniform and carried a pocket badge. Not that he did any undercover work; but it was simply useful to have someone who could make a call, or an inquiry, or deliver a message without having it appear to be a police matter.

"You know Ada Bronson?" Lanigan asked when the sergeant entered.

"Sure, Jim Bronson's wife."

"Well, find out where she is now. If she's home or where she's helping out."

"You want to see her, Chief? Should I bring her in, if she's free, I mean?"

"Yes, I want to talk to her, but don't bring her in. If she's free, ask her if she'd mind stopping by."

"Gotcha, Chief."

She came by shortly before noon. She was a woman of fifty, heavyset but surprisingly agile. Lumpy chin and almost lipless mouth were set in a worried frown. "Is it about Jim?" she asked.

"No, Ada," Lanigan said kindly. "Sit down, won't you. I want to ask you about last Wednesday. You were at the Millers', weren't you?"

"That's right. I was there all day on account it was before Thanksgiving. I got there maybe ten o'clock and made the missus her breakfast. Then I did some shopping and then I made us some lunch."

"But later in the afternoon—" Lanigan suggested.

"Oh, we was cooking and baking all afternoon. Then a little after five—see, I was listening to the early news at five—the phone rang, and it was the professor. He wanted to talk to his ma, but when I told him she was lying down, he said not to disturb her. Then he asked if Professor Kent had arrived, and I told him no. He said he must have gone straight to Breverton. Then he said he was taking the five thirty-two and would be home a little after six. See, he didn't drive into Boston, just to Swampscott, and took the train there on account of the snow."

"And what time did he get home?"

"Like he said, a little after six. But then just after he took his coat off, he was all upset because he'd left his bag on the train. And that upset the missus because she thought it was this fancy attaché case she'd given him last Christmas. But he said no, it was the old briefcase with the broken strap, that he wouldn't take the new case in this kind of weather. So then he had the missus look up the North station number and he phoned and told them he'd left his case on the train, and they said the conductor would take care of it when the train got to Gloucester. But he was terribly upset about it, and because he was, she was."

"And did the conductor find it? Do you know?"

"Yeah. I met the missus in the market Friday and she said he'd called and they had it. He wanted to go in and get it, but she wouldn't let him because he'd developed this terribly bad cold. Besides, there was no sense to it because if it was something he wanted to work on during the vacation, it was almost over."

"You've seen it, the bag, I mean?"

"Well, I never seen it, but over the phone he said it had his initials on it."

"All right, I guess he must have kept it in the trunk of his car. Were they expecting Professor Kent for Thanksgiving dinner? And were they disappointed when he didn't show?"

"Well, they were and they weren't. See, they thought he might drive down when the affair at the country club was over, and he'd stay the night and then have dinner with them the next day, and maybe stay until Monday morning. Which is why the missus had me do the guest room real nice. But they thought one of his fancy friends might invite him, and then he wouldn't come down."

"I see. And weren't they surprised when he didn't call to let them know one way or another?"

"Oh, he never calls. He just comes."

"And don't the Millers mind?"

"Well, they're from out west, you know, where I guess visiting is kind of free and easy. Besides, Professor Miller is a very obliging fellow. Before Professor Kent started coming to the house weekends, there was another professor who was engaged to a girl in town here, out in Charleton Park, and he'd go there for the weekend. Well, Professor Miller would drive him out there Friday afternoon and then go out there Monday morning to take him into Boston. Now, Charleton Park is quite a bit out of his way. It means going to Abbot Road and then driving around all those curvy streets in Charleton Park, but he didn't seem to mind. What's more, this fellow had a nine-o'clock class on Monday morning, and Professor Miller didn't have to get in until ten, but he'd get up early so as to get him in to his class on time."

"That was decent of him," Lanigan remarked. "You were helping out Mondays and Fridays?"

"The whole week. She was having trouble with her asthma, poor thing, so I'd come in every morning. Lately she's been feeling a little better, so I'd come in just when she felt she needed me. She's going off to visit her sister in Arizona at the end of the week. She was going to cancel when the professor came down with this cold, but he's better now, and wants her to go. She made him promise to stay home for the week, and I agreed to come in every day and do for him, so she'll be off Saturday."

"Uh-huh. Tell me, was Mrs. Miller interested in Professor Kent, or was she just being nice to him for her son's sake?"

"You mean was she sort of sweet on him? Well, she was a widow lady and he was a widower. And he was like high society, so-o for all that he was pretty old, I guess he was quite a catch, and if he'd asked her, she'd've said yes."

"Well, thank you, Ada," Lanigan said, and got up and escorted her to the door. At the door he said, "Oh, and there's no need to mention this little talk we've had to the Millers."

Chapter 36

Mrs. Bell was a practical, efficient woman of fifty-five. She reminded one of an old-fashioned schoolmarm who maintained discipline and brooked no nonsense. Indeed, she had once taught school, Domestic Science, in a small private school in the western part of the state. Then she had married, but the marriage was not a success. She discovered that her husband could not be trusted to keep sober, or out of debt, or even loyal to her, and she divorced him. Instead of going back to teaching, she began to do housework because it paid more.

When Matilda Kent began having difficulty in maintaining the house on Clark Street, the college engaged Mrs. Bell to help out. She would come in the late afternoon or early evening, straighten out the bedrooms, do some dusting, and prepare a high tea or an early supper for the couple. After Mrs. Kent died, she continued to do for Professor Kent. More often than not, Professor Kent was not at home when she came, but she had a key and let herself in. If he arrived while she was still there, she prepared his supper; otherwise she assumed he had eaten at a restaurant, and didn't bother.

She was sitting now in the office off the hallway, her hands primly folded in her lap, as Bradford Ames questioned her. "You got here at five o'clock last Wednesday? Was that your usual time?"

"Well, when Mrs. Kent was alive, I'd get here around four, or even earlier some days. That's because he'd come home at five and they'd have tea, sometimes a pretty elaborate tea with sandwiches and other stuff which I would prepare. High tea, he called it. I guess they wouldn't have supper then until maybe eight or nine o'clock. So I had everything fixed up nice for him when he came home."

"You'd serve the tea and wash up afterwards?" asked Ames.

"That's right. She'd have me put on a clean apron when I served, like a maid. I didn't mind. She was a nice old lady and it made her feel good."

"And afterwards, after she died?"

"Afterwards, I didn't come every day. I'd prepare his supper sometimes if he asked me to, and I'd wash the dishes afterwards. But more often he ate out. A lot of times he had this young Professor Miller over and they'd just sit around and talk and drink—"

"Drink?"

"Yes, beer if it was hot. Sometimes sherry or whiskey. Then I wouldn't hang around. I'd do my cleaning and leave."

Sergeant Schroeder, arms folded, leaning against the desk, asked, "Did he ever make a pass at you?"

Her small, thin lips relaxed in a reminiscent smile. "Once. He'd asked me to get him a cup of coffee. I was in the kitchen and had just brewed a pot. So I brought in a cup, and as I came to put it on the desk here, he leaned back and sort of stretched and he patted me on the behind."

"And what did you do?"

"I spilled the coffee on him."

"Accidentally?"

Again she smiled. "Accidentally on purpose."

Bradford Ames chuckled. "Weren't you afraid he'd fire you?"

She shook her head. "He couldn't fire me because he didn't hire me in the first place; the college did. And it was for his wife. All he could do was tell them he didn't need me. But then they wouldn't have hired anyone else. He'd have to do it on his own, and pay her on his own. If he told them he just wanted someone else, they'd probably ask me why. And I'd tell them. So I wasn't worried about getting fired."

"I see," said Ames. "Now, last Wednesday you came here at five o'clock."

"Yes."

"You're sure of the time?"

She nodded her head vigorously. "Oh yes. See, I charge by the hour, so I know exactly what time it is when I get to a job. I called earlier to say I was coming at five and—"

"You spoke to him? What time was that?"

"I called at five past four, right after finishing a job. He didn't answer, so I left a message on the answering machine. It's still there, I suppose," she said, nodding at the telephone on the desk. "I said I'd be here at five. And I was."

"Good enough," said Ames. "And he was gone when you got here?"

"That's right."

"How could you be sure?" asked Schroeder. "Couldn't he have been up in his bedroom? Did you go up to look?"

"I was there till seven. He didn't come down and I didn't hear anything. Besides, Professor Miller called at quarter past, past five, that is, and when I told him Professor Kent wasn't here, he asked me to go and look in the shed in back and see if his car was there."

"And was it?"

She shook her head. "No, it was gone. And I came back to the phone and told Professor Miller so. And he said he must have started out on his own."

"So he definitely left here by five," said Ames.

"Five past four if he didn't answer his phone when the lady here called," said Schroeder.

"But we can't be sure of that," said Ames. "He might have been busy and not want to answer. If he'd been dressing, for instance. If it were at all important, he was sure the caller would leave a message. Let's say five for certain, and four-thirty as probable."

"Do you want me to start cleaning up now?" she asked.

"No-o. I don't think so. And I don't want anything disturbed as yet. Don't bother to come in tomorrow, if you were planning to. We're still going over things, and I might want a few more pictures taken."

She glanced at her watch. "It's almost six, and I've been here since five. Can I charge for an hour?"

Ames looked at Schroeder. "Raises a fine ethical point, doesn't it, Sergeant? Does being interviewed by the police constitute work?"

"Well, it sure can't be called housework, which is what she gets paid for."

"But she came here to work, and we prevented her. You might even say we interrupted her in her work." He chuckled. "Yes, my dear, I think you can put in for an hour's work."

Chapter 37

I T was still bitter cold and the mounds of snow that the plows had thrown up on either side had narrowed the roads, in some places to half their width. But the highways, salted and sanded, were clear, although full of potholes. Driving was no fun, but Sergeant Schroeder felt he ought to question Baumgold. He had been in town Wednesday afternoon, and was planning to spend Thanksgiving with his wife in Barnard's Crossing, so why hadn't he picked her up at school or at her flat and gone there together? Or had he gone to the school and found she'd already gone? And had he, perhaps, taken the occasion to call on Professor Kent and tell him to keep his hands to himself?

Not surprisingly, considering the weather, Baumgold had no client at the time, and was sipping at a paper cup of coffee when he arrived. Sergeant Schroeder did not beat around the bush: after identifying himself, he put the question bluntly.

"Nope. I was at the courthouse until four or four-thirty and came straight home. Went right to Haymarket and was lucky enough to catch a bus right away."

"But you were going to spend Thanksgiving in Barnard's Crossing with your wife, so why didn't you pick her up and go out there together?"

"I would have if I had my car, but I didn't. I came in by bus."

"So . . ."

"So you remember the weather that afternoon. I live a couple of blocks from the bus stop. I could manage it all right, but I couldn't see her plowing through the snow for a couple of blocks. It was especially bad near where I live because I'm near the water."

"But she'd have to do it the next day if she was going to have dinner with you," Schroeder pointed out.

"No, she'd come in by train, and I'd meet her at Swampscott station in my car and drive her home."

"I would have thought you'd want her with you and she'd want to be with you for the whole vacation. Why didn't you stay over at her place Wednesday night and then you could have taken the train to Swampscott together the next day, that is, if you had to be in Barnard's Crossing?"

"Oh, we sure enough had to because we had a date to have dinner at a hotel and we'd already made reservations, but how would we have got from Swampscott to my place? It's too far to walk."

"You could have taken a cab."

"Oh yeah? You think it's like North station with a cab stand because of trains coming in every couple of minutes? If you want a cab, you've got to call, and then you wait—and wait—and wait. You call from a pay phone in this restaurant that's nearby, and I'm not even sure it was open Thanksgiving Day morning."

"Still, I should think where you're married less than a year, I understand—"

"That I'd want to be with her all the time?" Baumgold smiled condescendingly at the sergeant. "I suspect you've got a rather old-fashioned idea of marriage, Sergeant. Back in the days when a wife had no other interests than keeping house or taking care of children, couples tended to stay together as much as possible. It was the husband's duty to be with his wife because if she had children, she needed an adult to talk to at the end of the day, and if she didn't have children, she was bored out of her mind. But things are different nowadays. Wives work, and she has her own interests. I'm a lawyer and my wife is a teacher. She's involved with the college, and my work has little interest for her. We don't have to be together all the time, and we weren't even when we were in a relationship before we were married."

Schroeder was not used to being condescended to by the people he was questioning, and he changed the subject abruptly. "You knew Professor Kent?"

"I was introduced to him by Sarah, and I saw him a couple of times when I went to the English office to meet her when I came in to have dinner with her and stay over at her place. A dirty old man."

"I take it you didn't care for him."

"No, not one of my favorite people."

"You knew he'd made a pass at your wife a couple of times?"

"Yeah, she told me. I wanted to go see the old son of a bitch and tell him to keep his hands to himself, but Sarah wouldn't have it. That's another advantage of having your own work and your own interests: you learn how to take care of yourself."

"So if he'd seen you around last Wednesday and he'd asked you to drive him to Barnard's Crossing in his car, knowing you were going there, you wouldn't have accepted?"

Baumgold shrugged. "I might have, considering the weather. Sure, he was a bastard, but when I take the bus, do I know the driver is not another?"

❖   ❖   ❖

Disappointed in the results of his meeting with Baumgold, Schroeder thought he might yet justify—to himself—the long trip to the North Shore by dropping in at the Barnard's Crossing

Police Station, which was only ten or fifteen minutes away. Not that he had expected Baumgold to break down and confess, but he thought Baumgold might admit to having spoken to Kent; perhaps that he had been offered a ride to the North Shore. He would have felt the trip worthwhile if he had shown nervousness when questioned. It would have been a starting point for further investigation. But Baumgold had been perfectly at ease, had not even tried to conceal that he knew that Kent had been annoying his wife with his unwelcome attentions.

So if not Baumgold, who else might have driven to the North Shore with Kent? Bradford Ames had explained more than once that police in a small town like Barnard's Crossing knew everybody in town, that they were friends and neighbors and knew where they worked and their general habits.

When he entered the police station, Lanigan was out front talking to the desk sergeant. "I had to go to Salem," he explained, "so I thought I'd drop by on my way home to see if you had anything."

Lanigan shook his head. "No, nothing. We haven't been working on it since you people took over."

"I thought you know who in town here teaches at Windermere and might have got a ride with Kent."

"There's that Pendergast fellow," suggested the desk sergeant.

"Oh yeah. Where does he live?"

"He didn't go in the day before Thanksgiving," said Lanigan.

"How do you know?"

"Because I saw him in the supermarket when I stopped off to get some stuff for the missus around four o'clock."

"Oh. Anyone else?"

"As far as I can make out, not many teachers or students either have classes that late in the day. I was talking to John Aster, who's an engineer and teaches math at Windermere. According to him, he could make twice what he's getting there if he took an engineering job, but he'd have to work nine to five, and at the college he has only a couple of classes in the morning and he's free for the rest of the day."

"There's that fellow who comes out weekends," suggested the desk sergeant, "the one who comes to see the Lerner girl."

"Oh yeah," said Lanigan, "Jacobs, Morton; no, it's a biblical name, Mordecai. That's it: Mordecai Jacobs. Miller used to drive him out Friday afternoons and pick him up at the Lerners' Monday mornings. He lives in Brookline near Coolidge Corner."

❖   ❖   ❖

When, on his return to Boston, he reported on his trip to Salem, Ames's eyes widened in surprise. "You thought Baumgold might have killed him?"

"Well, Kent wanted to get to Miller's house in Barnard's Crossing, and he knew that Baumgold lived there, and Baumgold never did tell him off, so the old man didn't know how he felt about him—"

"So he offers him a ride, and on the way Baumgold kills him?"

"Well, he could have given him a dig in the ribs with his elbow while he was driving—"

"And that would have given Kent a heart attack? And Baumgold, a lawyer by profession, would have dropped him in the snow instead of notifying the police?"

"Well, we don't have a definite lead on anyone," said Schroeder sheepishly. "All we have is that Kent's car is gone. That's really all we have. So either Kent drove it and then parked it and took the bus, or someone drove him. Which means that someone didn't have the use of his own car that day."

"Or someone could have come in by car, parked it here in the city, and had it plowed in. And with the first thaw, he can come in by train or bus and get his car out and drive home, and no one the wiser," suggested Ames.

"Yeah, I guess that rabbi fellow is our prime suspect."

Ames shook his head. "I can't imagine a big, strapping young man like that actually violently attacking a little, scrawny old man like Kent."

"A big man is more likely to attack a little man than a little man is to attack a big man."

Ames chuckled. "That's very true, Sergeant. But if you recall, the basis for our taking over this case was that according to the autopsy, sketchy though it was, Kent was dead before he landed in the snow."

"Well, I was talking to a guy from the medical examiner's office, and according to him, determining time of death of somebody buried in snow for a couple of days can be pretty tricky business. There could be something like frostbite, which would then turn dark. And that might account for the discoloration on the buttocks."

"Yes, I suppose so," said Ames. "It's also possible that he started out a little after four o'clock, found the going a little harder than he expected, and drove to Haymarket, parked his car in a garage, and took the bus. Maybe if you questioned the bus drivers who left Haymarket for Barnard's Crossing after four—"

"I don't usually have much luck with bus drivers or streetcar conductors. They don't want to get involved. And at that hour there's usually a crowd getting on."

"But this man was in a tuxedo; he'd stand out in the crowd getting on."

"Yeah, but chances are in that weather he had his overcoat buttoned up to his chin."

"It wasn't buttoned up when he was found," Ames pointed out. "On the other hand, he was wearing patent leather pumps without rubbers or overshoes. As he stepped up, the bus driver was apt to notice and remember."

"You don't ride in buses much, do you? As passengers get on, the driver's eyes are glued to the coin box. But I'll contact the bus company anyhow. In the meantime, I've got another angle: fellow who lives right here in Brookline but goes to Barnard's Crossing every weekend to see his girl."

❖　❖　❖

The photo that Sergeant Schroeder showed Sam Patchek, the driver of the five-fifteen bus from Haymarket, had been doctored so that he was not lying in snow, but appeared to be standing and in good health. "Recognize this man? Was he on your bus the day before Thanksgiving?" He expected little and was agreeably surprised when the other said, "Oh, sure, I recognize him. He's on my bus every day. I didn't think he was as old as he looks in that picture. See, he always wears a hat; I didn't realize his hair was white."

"You're sure it's the one you know?"

"Oh, sure. See, he always wears a tuxedo. That's what makes him stick in my mind. I figured he was a waiter, or maybe a musician. I saw him yesterday. What's he done?"

❖　❖　❖

The driver from the five forty-five from Haymarket was African American, and truculent. "What's he say I done? I drove too fast? He was thrown off his feet when I went around a curve? Or I gave him the wrong change from a twenty-dollar bill? I don't give change at all."

"No, nothing like that. I just want to know if he was on your bus the day before Thanksgiving."

"Expect me to remember who got on my bus a week ago?"

"Well, he was in a tuxedo."

"So, I'm supposed to remember what kind suit, maybe what

kind tie, every guy gets on my bus is wearing? You know how many get my bus at Haymarket? I ride out with a full bus, standing room only. So what's his beef? What's he say I done?"

Chapter 38

THERE was an urgent note in Al Bergson's voice as he spoke to Rabbi Small on the telephone Thursday evening. "Look, David, I'd consider it a big favor if you and Miriam came out tomorrow to spend the Sabbath with us."

"It's not the kind of weather I care to drive in, and besides, the roads—"

"The roads are fine now. I had to go up to Gloucester, and the roads were fine. And the weather forecast for tomorrow is much warmer. It might go to forty."

"We-el—"

"Look, you can drive out in the early afternoon, turn the heat up in your house, and then come right over to our place. I'll try to get home early."

"Let me get back to you." To Miriam he said unnecessarily, "That was Al Bergson. He wants us to come out for the weekend."

"I figured. Why don't we, David?"

"Because he won't get home much before five. It's all right for you. You'll be with Edie in the kitchen, but what will I do?"

"I'll tell you what you can do, David. You can drop me off at the Bergsons' and then go on to the library. You can hang around there and read the magazines. Then come when Al will be getting home. We've been stuck here in the house all weekend—"

"All right, I'll tell him we're coming."

He left school right after his class, and after a bite of lunch, they started out. He was pleasantly surprised by how good the road conditions were. They made Barnard's Crossing in an hour, and Rabbi Small then went on to the library. He was curiously pleased that the librarian at the desk recognized him and smiled a greeting. He wandered about the magazine room, thumbing through the periodicals until he found an article that interested him, and then sat down in one of the large armchairs with which the room was furnished. It was not hard for him to spend a few hours in a library.

When he left, he first drove to his own house to see if it was comfortably warm from his having advanced the thermostat when they first arrived. Then he went on to the Bergson house, arriving at the same time as his host.

After the usual greetings, he asked, "Something bothering you, Al?"

"Yes, but I'd rather not discuss it in front of the women. We'll talk about it later, after the evening service, or even to-morrow. You won't mind riding to the temple if I drive, will you? It's pretty cold and not many of the sidewalks have been shoveled."

"Under the circumstances, I think we can ride."

Edie Bergson announced that she was tired and would not go. Miriam suspected that it was not so much that she was tired, but because she wanted to give the two men a chance to talk alone, so she said she'd stay and keep Edie company. It was a short trip to the temple from the Bergson house, offering little time for discussion.

"So what's bothering you?" asked the rabbi when they got into the car.

"I just want you to experience the Friday evening service. Then we'll talk."

When they entered the temple, several came over to greet the rabbi and to wish him the traditional good Sabbath. One asked, "You been sick, Rabbi? I haven't seen you around." Another asked, "Hey, how do you like teaching? College kids easier to deal with than a congregation?" One called to him, "Hi there, Teach." And one wanted to know if he should address him as Rabbi or Professor.

After the service, when the congregation went down to the vestry for tea or coffee and cake, Rabbi Selig approached him, wished him a good Sabbath, expressed his pleasure at seeing him, and then, dropping his voice, he asked, "Have you heard anything? Have you seen whatshisname, Lanigan?"

"No, I haven't heard from him, but he'll probably get in touch with me tomorrow night or Sunday. If he doesn't, I'll probably call him."

"How does he know you're here in town?"

"He may see my car in my driveway, or some member of the force will and tell him."

"You mean they watch your house?"

"Of course. Whenever you leave your house for a while—say you go on vacation—you fill out a form at the police station, and they make a point of keeping an eye on your place. I suppose they do in all small towns."

"I suppose that's if you live on a street. But what if you live on a hill some distance from the road; would they go up my driveway?"

"I doubt it. The cruiser would slow down as it passes your place. And they might go up and take a look around once in a while."

"I'll have to remember that. You fill out a form at the police station, eh? Very good." Again his voice dropped. "You'll let me know if Lanigan has anything, won't you?"

"Of course."

Ira Lerner approached the rabbi, tugged at his sleeve, and with a conspiratorial air motioned him to a small table in the corner. When they were seated, Lerner leaned forward and asked, "When a Boston cop comes here to Barnard's Crossing to—to make inquiries about someone living here, doesn't he have to check with our police first?"

"I don't know. I suppose he would as a matter of courtesy. Why?"

"Well, a Sergeant Schroeder came to my house and rang the bell. There was no one home except Maud, who does the housework. She's from Ireland, a country girl from Donegal and not too bright. She thought he had come about her status; see, she doesn't have a green card. Scared her half out of her wits. Well, it turned out it was me he wanted to see, so she told him I was in my office in Lynn. So what's he want of me? He wants to know when Mordecai Jacobs got to our house Thanksgiving, what time Wednesday he arrived."

"That so?"

"And when I tell him that he didn't come Wednesday, but came the next day, I sensed that he didn't believe me. See, Mord used to get a ride every Friday when he'd come out from a colleague, a Professor Miller who lives here in town. Nice fellow. And he'd pick him up Monday morning, too. Then something happened, I don't know what, and Miller couldn't or wouldn't give him a ride anymore. So Mord would come in by train, and Clara would pick him up at Swampscott station. Well, that Wednesday, when it was snowing so hard, Mord called and said he wouldn't be coming out the usual way because he didn't want

Clara driving in that kind of weather and maybe having to wait in the cold if the train was late; that he'd come out the next morning. Which he did. So what's it all about? Why does he want to know about Mord? I figure he must have checked with Lanigan, and—"

"You'd like me to ask Lanigan."

"That's right."

"All right, I'll try to see Lanigan sometime during the weekend. If he knows, and tells me, I'll let you know."

As they made their way to the car, Bergson demanded, "Well?"

"Well what?"

"Didn't you feel the tension? Didn't you notice the change in atmosphere?"

The rabbi shook his head. "It seemed like any other Friday evening service."

"Ah, David, you never had any sense of atmosphere. I tell you, the congregation is upset. There are rumors that the rabbi is planning to leave at the end of the year. And that worries a lot of people, even those who don't particularly like him. They think the Gentiles will take that as proof of guilt. And that wouldn't help the congregation in its dealings with the town, to have had a rabbi that was guilty of murder or manslaughter. And if he stays, it's maybe even worse, because here is a congregation whose leader is suspected of a serious crime, and they don't do anything about it."

"From what you say, I'm glad I have no sense of atmosphere. I'd be worried all the time. Look, Al, I don't for a moment think Rabbi Selig deliberately turned his snowblower on Kent and forced him off the ledge, but if he did it unwittingly because he didn't see him, then he is obviously not to blame. One couldn't even accuse him of carelessness because it was unlikely that anyone would venture on that right-of-way during the kind of storm we had. My advice would be not to worry about what you think the Gentiles might be thinking and—"

"There have been phone calls, David."

"So whatever was said is merely the opinion of the one person making the call. Look, Al, I'll try to see Lanigan. He'll know the feeling of the town if anyone does."

Chapter 39

Saturday, the weather began to return to normal for the time of year. At midday the temperature reached forty-two, which seemed almost springlike compared to the below-freezing weather that had been current for more than a week, ever since the day before Thanksgiving. The forecast for Sunday was that the temperature would be in the fifties and might even reach sixty. The snowbanks that lined the road, now blackened by the sand and grime thrown up by passing cars, was now beginning to melt, and there were puddles everywhere. In low-lying areas there were pools several inches deep where the melted water had collected, and as cars drove through, they tossed up sprays of dirty water, and cars going in the other direction had their windshields covered, momentarily blinding the drivers.

Sunday, David and Miriam had just finished their lunch when the phone rang. It was Lanigan. "David? Hugh Lanigan. Saw your car in the driveway. You here for the day?"

"And the night. I'm not due in Monday morning until eleven."

"Your car was seen in your driveway Friday afternoon, but it was not there during the evening, and then it was. I thought you didn't drive on your Sabbath."

"Well, I wanted to go to the temple, and walking was almost

impossible, especially for Miriam. We have an old fable about a famous rabbi who found himself in his carriage on the road when the Sabbath fell. So he ruled that it was Sabbath everywhere except where his carriage was; that there it was still a weekday. So I thought I'd make the same ruling."

"It's a good trick. Maybe I'll get you to do it for me when Town Meeting rolls around and I find myself having to do a week's work in one day."

"Look, Chief, I want to see you."

"Well, I'm tied down here at the station house until five. Why don't you come down here and—"

"Fine. But Miriam is here and—"

"Tell you what, David, you come down here and we'll talk. Then we'll go to your place and pick up Miriam and you'll come to my house. I'll call Amy and tell her you're coming over for the evening. She baked some doughnuts. We'll have coffee and doughnuts and I'll give you a drink."

"Sounds fine. I'll be down in a few minutes."

"See, I cleared my desk for you," said Lanigan as Rabbi Small entered his office.

"That's very decent of you, Chief. I didn't mean to interrupt your work."

Lanigan grinned. "Nah, I didn't have anything to do, but I'm on duty one Sunday a month, and this is it. I called Amy and she's expecting us. Now, what's bothering you?"

"This business of Professor Kent, of course. I talked to Rabbi Selig Friday night. He's been getting phone calls, and so has Al Bergson, and others, too."

"David, David, you've seen letters in the newspaper from crazy people. Well, for every letter there are a hundred phone calls. To write a letter you at least have to know how to write. You need paper. You need a stamp. And anything you say is there in black and white so it can't be denied later. But to make a phone call, all you have to do is lift the receiver. No reasonable person believes that the young rabbi deliberately pushed Kent off the ledge. Besides, Bradford Ames is convinced he was dead before he got here."

"So that's why Sergeant Schroeder questioned Ira Lerner about his daughter's friend, Mord Jacobs."

"Did he now?"

"Yes, and Lerner said he seemed to doubt whatever he told him."

"Ah, David, that's just Schroeder's way. If his salary had to be passed on every year by a town meeting, he'd be a lot friendlier in dealing with the citizens who do the voting."

"Did you know he was going to question Lerner? Did he check with you?"

Lanigan shook his head. "He may have stopped by and spoken to the desk sergeant."

"You mean you're out of it completely?"

"Pretty much. Ames asked me to interview a Tony Donofrio in Lynn, but that's probably because he didn't want him subjected to the Schroeder type of interview."

The outside phone rang, and as he reached for it, Lanigan said, "That's probably Amy to tell me to pick up something at the supermarket."

But it wasn't. It was Bradford Ames. "I called your house, but your wife said you were on duty at the station house."

"Yeah, one Sunday a month—"

"Look, Chief, we found Kent's car. It was parked on Blossom Street, in Lynn."

"That's right near the train station."

"Right. And Tony Donofrio and his wife occupy a flat on that street. Sergeant Schroeder thinks if we pull him in and question him for a while, we might get something interesting. Now, you questioned Donofrio, so I'd like to talk to you about him. I'm here in Barnard's Crossing in my place on the Point. If you could come over—"

"I'm here with Rabbi Small. You remember him, don't you?"

"Oh, sure, I certainly remember Rabbi Small. Look, have him come, too."

"But he's here with his wife. And my wife is expecting him and his wife for the evening."

"Oh, I see. Well, how about tomorrow morning? Will you be free? Can you come in to Boston, say at ten, not at my office, but at Kent's house next to the college? I've made it my temporary headquarters while we go through his stuff."

"I guess I can make it."

Chapter 40

ALTHOUGH they were ready to leave by eight o'clock, the rabbi puttered around, and Miriam, sensing that he was reluctant to drive to Boston while traffic was at its heaviest, suggested that they have another cup of coffee. It was half past before they finally set out.

"You taking the old Boston Road, David?" she asked.

"No, I'll take the State Road; road conditions are apt to be better." And that was the last they spoke while he leaned forward, his hands clutching the steering wheel until they reached their apartment in Brookline and he parked in his usual place along the car tracks. He boarded the streetcar that took him to Kenmore Square, walked the few short blocks to the college, and noted that it was not yet ten when he reached his office.

He had no sooner hung his coat on the rack than there was a knock on the partly open door. He called, "Come in," and noted with surprise that it was Bradford Ames who entered.

"I was hoping to find you in, Rabbi," said Ames. "I'd like you to join us at Kent's house."

"Why? I gathered from Hugh Lanigan that you were going to talk about Donofrio. I never met the man. I know nothing about him."

"Well, yes, I wanted to talk about Donofrio, but I also wanted to talk about all aspects of the case, all we know, and it occurred to me that you knew Kent—"

"Just barely."

"But the rest of us didn't know him at all. And you know the college, the atmosphere— Why are you laughing?"

"I came out to Barnard's Crossing at the urging of Al Bergson, the president of the temple. He wanted me to note the change in the Friday evening service. When I told him that I had seen no change, he told me that I had no sense of atmosphere. And here you want me to come to your meeting as an expert on the atmosphere of the college."

"You know what I mean. The gossip, the talk—"

"The departments don't fraternize much."

"Yes, but you hear talk in the cafeteria when you have lunch—"

"I bring my lunch. But I do go to the cafeteria for a cup of coffee now and then. Sometimes alone, sometimes with Mord Jacobs, or Roger Fine—you remember him—sometimes with Sarah McBride, all from the English Department. Sometimes Dr. Cardleigh, the dean, joins me for a cup of coffee with his pipe."

"Well, there you are, Rabbi; you've at least met Professor Kent, and you've occasionally had coffee with various members of his department. So why don't you put your coat on and come across the street to Kent's house with me?"

"All right, I'll be happy if I can be of any use. Something tells me this might take a while, so I'll leave a note on the door saying I won't meet my class today."

❖   ❖   ❖

There was a uniformed policeman who was sitting on one of the kitchen chairs just inside the door who admitted them. They repaired to the study and deposited their overcoats on the couch and then sat down to await the arrival of Schroeder and Lanigan. Schroeder arrived a minute or two later. He said, "Good morning," and then with a nod in the rabbi's direction, he asked, "What's he doing here?"

Ames chuckled. "I thought he might be useful. He'd met Kent, and he knows the college. Besides, I'm sure you remember how useful Rabbi Small was the last time we were involved with the college."

Lanigan arrived soon after. He was carrying a battered old briefcase, which he deposited on the floor beside his chair. "Sorry I'm late," he said. "I stopped off—"

"It's all right, Chief," said Ames. "Let's get started. We might as well stay here; it's the most comfortable room in the house and the only one besides the kitchen that's properly heated. I suspect that Kent spent most of his time here. Some of his clothes are in that closet, and I wouldn't be surprised if he slept on that couch at times. I'll have to ask Mrs. Bell." He opened a drawer of the desk and took out a sheet of paper. "All right, let's see what we've got. When was Kent last seen alive?"

Schroeder flipped the leaves of his notebook. "He was in the school, just leaving to come here to finish dressing for this party he was going to."

"Who saw him?"

"His friend Miller, who was in the English office, and Ms. McBride, who came in just as he was leaving."

"All right," said Ames. "Now, Mrs. Bell said she called at five past four, and there was no answer. I have the feeling that when Mrs. Bell says she called at four-oh-five, that was exactly when she called. There was no answer, which I assume means that he hadn't got home yet. When next did someone try to make contact with him?"

"Donofrio took the train in Lynn at three-forty," said Lanigan. "He said he came straight here and rang and knocked on the door. If the streetcar to Kenmore came right away, it would still be around half past four, because the three-forty out of Lynn gets to North station at four-o-two."

"Then he came to the English office and spoke to Professor Sugrue," said Schroeder after a glance at his notebook. "Asked if Kent might be teaching. And when told that he wasn't, went back to knock on the door again. Figured Kent might have been busy or been in the john when he knocked the first time. When Mrs. Bell came at five o'clock, the house was empty. Professor Miller called at a quarter past, and she told him Kent was not there. He had her look in the garage in back, and sure enough, the car was gone. So I figure that Donofrio is our man. I spoke to him after we found the car on his street, and he was pretty nervous."

It occurred to the rabbi that almost anyone might be nervous when Schroeder questioned him, but he said nothing. Lanigan, however, remarked, "I spoke to him and he didn't seem the least bit nervous."

"From what you told us of your conversation with him, I thought I'd better have a talk with him when Kent's car turned up on his doorstep, so to speak," said Schroeder. The implication was that the amateur having opened the door, it was time for the professional to step in. "He wasn't too willing to talk to me; said he'd told you everything. When I pointed out that the car was found on his street, he claimed he knew nothing about it. My guess is that he parked and then went off to booze it up with his buddies, and forgot all about it. He admitted that he got home pretty late. Or maybe when he got back to move it, he found it plowed in and couldn't."

"Seems to me," Lanigan offered, "that if I had a hot car, my street would be the last place I'd park it."

"Sure," the sergeant agreed, "but with the storm we had that Wednesday, it wasn't easy to find a parking place, so he took the first one that showed up. But it wasn't just the car on his street that made me suspicious of him. See, we checked Kent's safe-deposit box, and it had an insurance policy of fifty thousand dollars, and the beneficiary was Donofrio's wife. There was also a will leaving everything to Donofrio's daughter. And what with a savings account and a checking account, there was over twenty thousand that he had in the bank, plus other property that he might have. To Donofrio some seventy thousand dollars would be a pretty good reason for wanting him dead."

"Is that all that was in the safe-deposit box?" asked the rabbi.

"Oh, there was some jewelry and there was a doctor's dissertation on—"

"Simeon Suggs, whom I've never heard of," said Ames.

"Aha!"

Ames turned to the rabbi. "And what does that 'Aha' portend? Is it rabbinical or merely professorial?"

"It's neither." He laughed. "But my first day here I met with the dean, Dr. Cardleigh, who talked of the stupidity of requiring a dissertation for the Ph.D. His own degree is an M.D., by the way. It takes two or three years to do one, and since it had to be original, it was usually about a subject that wasn't worth doing. He mentioned that someone here had written on Simeon Suggs, a poet he'd never heard of. I didn't like to inquire, but I've wondered off and on which member of the English Department it was. Now I know it was Professor Kent.

"But it wasn't Professor Kent's dissertation, Rabbi. It was a photocopy issued by a microfilm company in Michigan that specializes in that sort of thing. It was written by—er—Sergeant?"

Schroeder, grinning at the idea of scoring off the rabbi, thumbed his notebook and announced, "Oscar Horton, University of Nevada, 1953."

"Hmm." The rabbi stared up at the ceiling in disregard of the smiles on the faces of the others. Then he lowered his gaze and said, "Then I am prepared to make a wager."

Ames emitted a gurgly chuckle. "All right, Rabbi, you're covered. What's your bet?"

"I am willing to bet that Professor Miller is the one Dr. Cardleigh referred to."

"You mean—"

"I mean that Professor Miller copied that Horton dissertation and submitted it as his own. And further, that Kent found out about it somehow and used it to coerce Miller."

"To do what?"

"Anything he asked of him; to invite him to his house in Barnard's Crossing practically every weekend, to be his chauffeur, to be his constant companion. Kent was a bore whom no one liked. His colleagues were leery of him, even feared him because of his influence with the trustees through his wife, Matilda Clark. Friendless and alone, he forced Miller to be his friend. The Odd Couple, they called them. He even got Miller tenure, to be sure that he'd stay on at Windermere."

"Are you suggesting that Miller might have killed him?" asked Ames.

The rabbi nodded. "Mm-hm. I think it very likely. I suspect he was going to leave him here in the house, because he assumed the body would not be found until Monday at the earliest. But then he discovered that the housekeeper was coming in at five. He didn't answer the phone when she called, but he played it back on the answering machine, and he knew she had a key. So he brought the body out to the car in the garage."

"No way, David," said Lanigan. "It's a pretty theory, but it's wrong because Miller took the five thirty-two from North station. There's no way he could have driven out to Barnard's Crossing and back between four o'clock and five thirty-two."

"How do you know he did?"

"Because he left his bag on the five thirty-two. He called the Baggage Department at North station as soon as he got home. I

234

was late coming here this morning because I stopped off on my way to get it. I thought I'd bring it to him and use the occasion to ask him who might have had it in for Kent."

"That's the bag?" asked Ames, pointing to where it was resting on the floor.

"Uh-huh. His initials are on it."

"It seems a pretty shabby sort of bag," said Ames. "One strap is torn off and the buckle seems to be ripped, and it's all scratched up. It looks as though it had been kicking around in the trunk of a car."

"I suppose it's what's in it that was so important to him," said Lanigan.

"What *is* in it?" asked Ames impatiently. "It's not locked, is it?"

"No, it's not locked. You want me to look in it?"

"Go ahead."

Lanigan opened the bag and drew out a copy of the Boston *Herald* dated Wednesday, the twenty-third. He fished in it with his hand and, shaking his head, said, "That's all there is, just the *Herald.*"

"Why was he so anxious about a newspaper that he could get at any newsstand?" asked Schroeder.

"To fill it out," said the rabbi. "If it were empty, you might wonder why he was so anxious to retrieve it."

"I suppose," Ames admitted, "but it does prove that he was on the five thirty-two."

"If that's its sole purpose," the rabbi remarked, "then it proves that he wasn't."

"That sure makes a lot of sense," said Schroeder, his voice heavy with sarcasm. "You saying that if I can prove I did something, it proves I didn't?"

"Are you suggesting he had someone else leave it there for him?" asked Lanigan.

The rabbi nodded. "Possible, but just barely. You mean he

might have met a student going to Swampscott or Salem and asked him to leave his bag on one of the overhead racks of the train? But the student would surely talk, mention it to a friend." He shook his head. "No, not at all likely. We've got to go back a step." His voice took on a Talmudic singsong. "I-if the bag proves he was on the five thirty-two, the-en what in turn does that prove?"

Ames glanced at Lanigan, his eyes twinkling as he asked, "You going to give us some of that Talmudic reasoning that you called pul-pul or something?"

"Pul-pil, he calls it," said Lanigan.

"It's called *pil-pul*," said the rabbi, "which is the Hebrew for pepper. It denotes making fine distinctions, which you might call hairsplitting. The rabbis of old who developed it were engaged in finding the true meaning of one of God's commandments. They had all the time in the world and they weren't worried if an argument was far-fetched as long as it contributed to their understanding. Now, in the present case, the bag proves he was on the five thirty-two. But that is important only because it implies that he was in Boston's North station at half past five so that he could board the train, which left two minutes later. And that would mean that he couldn't have dropped off the body of Kent in Barnard's Crossing and got back to Boston in time to catch the five thirty-two.

"Bu-ut . . ." And once again his voice took on the Talmudic singsong. "The train stops along the way. And one of the places it stops is Lynn. It gets there about twenty minutes later, and the Lynn station is only about ten minutes from Swampscott or Barnard's Crossing. He had plenty of time to get to Lynn after he had dropped off the body of Kent behind the billboard. My guess is, he went to Swampscott station where his car was parked first, got the bag out of the trunk, then drove to Lynn in Kent's car, parked it on Blossom Street, and then walked to Lynn station. There he bought a newspaper, stuffed it into his bag, and boarded the train, the five thirty-two."

"When were you planning to bring the bag to Miller, Chief?" asked Ames.

"Oh, sometime this evening."

"All right. I'm going to see this Dr. Cardleigh, and if the rabbi is right about the dissertation, I'd like to come with you when you go to see Miller."

"Sure, come to the station house and we'll go from there."

Ames turned to the rabbi. "And how much were you betting, Rabbi?"

"I hadn't thought about it. Would a dollar be about right?"

Ames gurgled a chuckle. "A dollar it is. You're faded, Rabbi."

Chapter 41

THORVALD Miller himself, fully clothed, opened the door to them.

"You better?" asked Lanigan.

"Well, my temperature is down, so I got out of bed."

"And your ma?"

"Oh, she's off to Arizona to visit her sister."

"This is Bradford Ames," said Lanigan. "He's assistant district attorney for Suffolk County. He's got a place on the Point. We were visiting and he thought he'd come along when I said I had to return your briefcase."

"Oh, good. You brought it."

"Yes. Here it is. Tell me, what was there in the *Herald* that made you so anxious to get it back from the railroad?"

"You opened it?"

"Yes, we opened it. And all that was in it was the day's *Herald*."

"Well, there was an editorial—"

"You bought it in Lynn?" asked Lanigan.

"After you parked the car on Blossom Street near the station," suggested Ames.

"Somebody claims they saw me? Was it the newsstand fellow?"

"No, but you couldn't get back to Boston in time to take the five thirty-two, not from Barnard's Crossing," said Lanigan.

Suddenly Miller relaxed. He even smiled. "Then you know."

"Yes, we know," said Lanigan.

"Why did you kill him?" Ames asked. "Was it because of the thesis?"

"And just how did you do it?" asked Lanigan.

Miller laughed, and Ames thought he detected a note of hysteria in the laugh. "As to how, I tied his bow tie very, very tight. It seemed appropriate because that's how he first approached me, asked me to tie his bow tie. And then in gratitude insisted I come to his place for a drink. That's when he showed me the copy of the Horton dissertation. As to why, because he was blackmailing me. Oh, not for money. I don't have any to speak of. But for companionship and service. I had to spend practically every afternoon with him. And if he had a fancy affair in the evening, I'd have to help him get dressed, like kneeling down to put his shoes on. When he'd come here, we'd take his car and he'd have me drive. So I was chauffeur and butler and valet to him. He got me tenure to make sure I wouldn't be dropped and go someplace else. There's a job in Arizona that I had a chance at. It's only a junior college, a technical school at that, but when I told him I wanted to take it because Arizona would be good for my mother's asthma, he said that they'd be sure to ask for references from Windermere and he'd hear about it and write to them about the dissertation. So I figured I was stuck here until he died, and that could be a long time. So I knew I had to do something about it."

"You planned to do it the day before the vacation so he wouldn't be found until Monday four or five days later," Ames suggested.

"That's right. I knew I had to get him out of there. I put his coat on him and was going to get his rubbers, but somebody came to the door, and if I went to get his rubbers in the hallway, I might be seen. The person at the door knocked and then waited and knocked again and then again. So I walked him out the back door, like you walk a drunk. His car had a seat belt and a shoulder belt that came down automatically when you closed the door, so I wasn't worried about his falling forward or sliding off his seat if I put on the brakes."

"That accounts for the discoloration on thighs and buttocks," Ames said in an aside to Lanigan.

"My idea was to drop him off the road at some wooded place, but when I got on the State Road, I found that there were snow mounds three and four feet high on either side and plenty of cars coming along in spite of the storm. So then I decided to swing over to the old Boston Road when I got to Barnard's Crossing and drop him off behind that billboard. I swear it wasn't to get that rabbi fellow involved."

"And what were you going to do with the car?" asked Lanigan.

"I realized I couldn't leave it there because then the question would be why he didn't drive up Evans Road if he were coming here to my house. What came to mind then was to drive to Swampscott station and swap his car for mine. But that wasn't too good either because the police would be able to check the few local cabs, and besides, would a cabbie drop him off at the billboard instead of taking him here? He certainly couldn't walk from the station to my house.

"But when I got to the station it wasn't quite half past five. That meant that I could drive to Lynn, park somewhere near the Lynn station, and board the five thirty-two there because it didn't get there until almost six. Then I thought I'd leave something on the train to prove I was on it. I had an old pile of junk in the trunk of my car in a large trash bag that I was planning to drop off at the Salvation Army depot first chance I got. But it was shoes, pants, shirts, an old sweater—nothing you could leave on a train. And the crummy old briefcase. Nobody would make a fuss over a briefcase like that, so I had to fill it. With what? I had nothing in my car, no papers, no books, no magazines. So I bought a paper and stuffed that in." He grinned broadly. "And just in case somebody should pinch it, thinking there was something worthwhile in it, when I got off the train at Swampscott, I told the fellow whose car was next to mine that I had left my briefcase on the train. I didn't know him, but I'd seen him around. I memorized the number on his license plate so if necessary I could locate him. Seven-two-three-CBE. It's an easy number to remember because it rhymes."

"You realize you're confessing to murder," said Ames gravely.

"Not murder," said Miller, "justifiable homicide. No jury is going to convict me when they hear how he treated me, especially the part about my ma."

"Yes, you've got a good chance, the way murder trials have been going in this state lately," said Ames, "but you could be found guilty of second- or third-degree murder and have to do time."

"So I'd do some time, but when I got out I'd be free."

"Look, with your mother gone, you're alone here, and you shouldn't be since you've been sick."

"I'm all right now. It was a twenty-four-hour flu."

"Still, there could be a recurrence. I suggest you come down to the station house and stay there for a while. There's always somebody there."

"Are you arresting me?"

"Let's just say we're taking you into protective custody. So pack what you're going to need for the next couple of days and we'll go along."

"All right."

"Why don't we just arrest him?" asked Lanigan as Miller left the room.

"Because we didn't read him his Miranda rights, and a smart lawyer could make something of it. Down at the station house we'll read him his rights and have him make his confession to a stenographer who'll type it up and we'll have him sign it."

Chapter 42

THE rabbi had just drawn a cup of coffee and sat down at a table in the cafeteria when Dean Cardleigh approached puffing at his pipe, a coffee cup in hand. He sat down opposite the rabbi.

"I didn't read Miller's dissertation through by any means. I read a chapter or two because I wondered how anyone could spend two or three years of his life working on such tripe. We have it somewhere in the archives if you want to have a look at it. You know, if I were not a dean with all the duties thereunto pertaining as they say in diplomas, I'd be inclined to applaud Miller for having the good sense to copy his dissertation instead of wasting his time doing the research and the writing of it."

That bad, was it?

"This Suggs wrote some occasional verse, filler stuff for magazines and newspapers. He worked for his father-in-law, who was a printer. Some people who later became sort of important came there to have their work printed and published at their own expense. But they never said anything noteworthy to him, or if they did, he never noted it in his diary. Believe me, it wasn't worth the two hundred and eighty pages of paper it was written on."

"But wasn't he hired on the basis of it?"

Cardleigh laughed. "He was hired because we needed an English teacher at the time. And our silly rules at the time required a Ph.D. And the even sillier rules of the Ph.D. require an original dissertation that no one ever reads." He puffed at his pipe, found that it had gone out, and lit another match. "An interesting case of one faker imposing on another."

He tamped down his pipe, took a sip of coffee, and leaned back in his chair. "Tim Bishop was a textbook salesman who used to drop in on me whenever he was in the area, although I never changed the textbook of Greek Literature that I was using. One day, after I had become dean, he came into my office and said, 'I see you've got Mike Canty teaching for you.' I told him we didn't have a Michael Canty on the faculty. And he answered, 'I saw him in Room 103 as I came down the corridor.'

"So I looked at my chart and said, 'That was Professor Malcolm Kent in 103.' To which he answered that he must have changed his name. He was sure it was Mike Canty, who'd worked at the International Correspondence School of St. Louis when he'd worked there. And according to Bishop, he'd been merely a clerk and had never been to college. He'd gone to London when they opened an office there, Canty or Kent had. And on the basis of when the office in London closed and when he started teaching here, he couldn't have gone to college, let alone acquired a master's degree.

"I mentioned it to one of the trustees I was friendly with, and he was aghast. He was afraid that if the story got out, it would ruin the reputation of the college. He thought that anyone that Kent had flunked might even be able to sue the college. So I kept quiet about it. After all, I had no proof; only Bishop's word.

"On my next sabbatical, my wife and I went to England, and I checked it out. And Bishop was right: no Kent or Canty at either place. But there wasn't anything I could do about it since Kent was now married to Matilda Clark. I felt I ought to tell President Macomber at least, but I decided not to. He's such a straight arrow that he'd be sure to want to do something about it and would get into a row with the Board of Trustees. And between a president who can be readily replaced and several million dollars of endowment, there's no question which the Board would choose. If I told him, it might very well cost him his job." He took a long swig of his coffee. "You might say that in approving the listing in the catalog of Malcolm Kent, M.A., University of Liverpool, I was also a faker." He chuckled. "I suppose a bit of skulduggery is endemic to every institution. But now it's over. Another cup of coffee, Rabbi?"

About the Author

Harry Kemelman is the author of the hugely popular Rabbi Small mystery series, which includes *Sunday the Rabbi Stayed Home, Monday the Rabbi Took Off, Tuesday the Rabbi Saw Red, Wednesday the Rabbi Got Wet, Thursday the Rabbi Walked Out, Friday the Rabbi Slept Late, Saturday the Rabbi Went Hungry, One Fine Day the Rabbi Bought a Cross, Someday the Rabbi Will Leave,* and *The Day the Rabbi Resigned.* There are almost seven million copies of Rabbi Small mysteries in print.

Harry Kemelman lives in Marblehead, Massachusetts.